"I wish there was music tonight."

Mel's voice was rough with feeling as he drew her close. "I'd like to dance with you again."

"We could pretend there's music," Verna murmured, caressing his face with her fingertips.

Mel held out his arms. Cheek to cheek, they began to sway in the same rhythm, to the same inaudible music. *I'm in heaven*, Verna thought dreamily.

With almost imperceptible moves Mel danced them over to the bedroom door. Verna reached up and nibbled on his lower lip, tantalizing him.

"It's been a perfect day, Verna. Is there any reason it has to end?"

Against his mouth she whispered, "No reason at all . . ."

Mary Jo Territo decided it would be fun to write a book about two people who share a problem that can be remedied before the book's conclusion. A great cook, she also loves to write about food. This humorous, warm tale of Verna and Mel is sure to touch your heart and tease your palate.

Before becoming a writer, Mary Jo worked in the theater and as an editor. She lives in Bronxville, New York, with her husband.

Books by Mary Jo Territo

HARLEQUIN TEMPTATION
52–JUST FRIENDS
111–CATCH A RISING STAR
121–THE VITAL INGREDIENT
142–NO PASSING FANCY

HARLEQUIN SUPERROMANCE
190–TWO TO TANGO

Before and After

MARY JO TERRITO

Harlequin Books

TORONTO • NEW YORK • LONDON
AMSTERDAM • PARIS • SYDNEY • HAMBURG
STOCKHOLM • ATHENS • TOKYO • MILAN

Published November 1987

ISBN 0-373-25280-3

Prologue

FRIDAY NIGHT. Nine o'clock. Congress had adjourned until mid-January, and Capitol Hill was like a deserted army camp. Only Verna Myers was holding down the fort at her desk in the Russell Senate Office Building. She was very tired, but the pile of finished files was at last higher than the unfinished stack. She should be on her way home by eleven or twelve, she thought, and then she would have four weeks of blessed freedom. Four whole weeks without a law abstract to read, a meeting to attend, a report to write. Just thinking about her vacation gave her the push she needed to slog on and finish her work.

She took a bite out of the giant roast-beef sandwich on her desk and pulled a handful of potato chips out of the large bag beside it. She devoured the chips at the rate of about two per paragraph as she read through one of the many abstracts that pertained to the proposed Carlsen-Byram Agriculture Act. The new farm bill had been her senator's main concern during the legislative session just concluded. The issue was so complex, however, that the bill had not even gotten to committee before the adjournment. So Verna looked ahead to many more months of deep involvement in agricultural policy when she returned to Washington. Despite the intricacy and frequent tedium of the work, the prospect of doing more of it held nothing but excitement for her, an excitement that only partly stemmed from being a farmer's daughter and a public servant of the state of Iowa.

"Burning the midnight oil, Verna?"

She looked up to see James J. Byram, congressman of Kansas and cosponsor of the farm bill, standing in the doorway. As always Jim looked fresh and crisp despite the long hours he had worked. Verna knew he was in his office by seven, and that was after he'd run his daily six miles in Rock Creek Park. She often wondered when the man slept, a bit of information she would be happy to glean firsthand.

"I'm going on vacation tomorrow, and after that I'll be at the senator's office in Des Moines for a month. I've been working extra late every night this week to get everything sorted out."

"I didn't realize you were going to be away. Mind if I come in?" He waved a sheaf of papers at her. "These are for Aggie. I was going to slip them under the door so she'd find them in the morning—"

"Tomorrow's Saturday," Verna reminded him.

"And we both know that means she'll be here earlier than usual. Can you make sure they're in a place where she'll see them?" He smiled the winning smile that made him Washington's hottest new political commodity, as well as its most eligible bachelor. Verna was quite aware of his qualifications for both those honorary positions.

Jim put the papers on her desk, then pulled up a chair and sat down opposite her. Verna saw him look askance at the bag of chips and the roast-beef sandwich oozing mayonnaise. She knew James J. Byram's feelings about healthy foods and regular exercise only too well. He was vocal enough about them. And she had to admit that rabbit food and running had done Jim Byram no harm at all. There wasn't an excess ounce on his lean six-foot frame. His blond hair was thick, straight and shining, his dark-blue eyes were clear and sparkling and his skin had a golden touch of tan all through the year.

Verna looked guiltily at her food and wished she could hide it in a desk drawer. Or, better yet, sweep it into the trash can. But that would only draw more attention to it. She said coolly, "I have to call the senator in the morning. I'll make sure she knows they're here."

With the intensity for which he was quickly becoming famous, Jim launched into a discussion of the finer points of the farm bill. Verna listened and took notes, knowing that she would stay even later now to write a memo to Senator Carlsen. But even as she worked, her mind wasn't first and foremost on the farm bill. It was first and foremost on the bill's cosponsor.

What would it take for Jim Byram to notice that she cared for more than the farm bill where he was concerned? That she had other qualities besides those that made her a crack legislative aide and Agatha Carlsen's political protégée? That she was a woman, one who knew his professional world very well and who wanted to know his personal world intimately?

Just wait until I get back, she vowed silently. *Congressman James J. Byram is not going to be able to keep his eyes off me. Or his hands.*

Jim finished talking about the farm bill. "Where are you going on your vacation?"

"South Carolina," she told him. "Hilton Head Island."

"Nice," he commented. "I've never been there myself, but I hear the beaches are spectacular. You know, walking on the beach is good for—" he paused diplomatically "—what ails you."

She skirted the remark just as diplomatically. She knew exactly what "ailed" her. It stared back at her in the mirror every morning. "How would someone from Kansas know that?" she asked lightly.

"The same way that someone from Iowa would," he countered. He propelled himself out of the chair with his customary jet-engine energy. "I don't know what Aggie's going to do without you for a whole month."

"I'm sure she'll manage," Verna said modestly.

"Aggie might. She can manage anything. But what about us lesser mortals? I suppose we'll muddle through somehow." He paused and gave her a broad smile, making his eyes crinkle in that way Verna found irresistible. "Have a wonderful time, Verna. I'll miss you. G'night." He tipped her a salute and loped out of the room.

Her hand flew to the base of her throat. She could feel her heart pounding in her chest. That was the most personal thing he'd ever said to her. He *did* notice her. He *did* appreciate her. Still, for all those months she'd felt like a last drab forlorn box of soap powder in the supermarket where he was concerned. But those days were nearly over. When she returned with her new packaging, he surely would grab her right off the shelf.

Of all the beautiful, talented women who clamored after him, she would be the one he'd choose. After his parting smile she was confident of that.

Has there ever been a husband-and-wife team in Congress? she wondered as she reached for the papers Jim had brought. With the other hand she reached for another handful of chips. Then she thought better of it and swept the bag into the trash. A second later she had wrapped up the remains of her sandwich and deposited them there, too. Who needed food when there were smiles like Jim Byram's to dine on?

1

ON SUNDAY MORNING Verna passed through the gates of the Last Resort. She was feeling jittery and had been all morning, which was understandable. She was about to take a very big step in her life. She pulled her car off the road and peered speculatively down the long avenue flanked with stately live oaks. With their gray beards of Spanish moss swaying in the gentle sea breezes, the trees seemed to be benevolent grandfathers, urging her on. There was no need to be nervous, she reassured herself. Everything was going to be fine.

She pressed in the clutch of her snappy red compact and pushed the gear lever into first. As she eased the clutch out and slowly pulled back onto the road, she heard a sudden loud honk. A chocolate-brown Jaguar swerved around her and raced down the road like an angry roadrunner. Her car stalled with a jolt.

"I thought this place was supposed to be relaxing," she muttered as she shifted into Neutral and turned the key in the ignition. The car coughed daintily, as if miffed by such rude treatment, and turned over reluctantly. Verna pressed lightly on the gas pedal until the car was purring smoothly and continued down the road.

At the end of the oak-lined drive there was a long, low building sided with gray-stained wood that blended with the beauty of the subtropical island environment. Behind the building she spied a sparkling sliver of blue-green sea. Though it was late October, the temperature was in the mid-seventies and the ocean was a welcome and inviting sight. She'd come just the ninety miles from Charleston that morning, but Saturday's drive from Washington had been long and tiring—and lonely. With every mile, Jim's Friday-night farewell grew more and more distant. One smile and an "I'll miss you" did not make a budding relationship. Even if she looked like a million-dollar, no-strings-attached campaign contribution when she returned to Washington, he still might treat her like "good old Verna." Then again he might not, she thought, doubling her resolve to put her many failures behind her and succeed at the Last Resort.

She pulled into a parking spot, careful to take the one farthest from the Jaguar, which, she noted irritably, had hogged two spaces. *Well*, she told herself philosophically, *come to a place like this and you're bound to run into piggish behavior.* She climbed out of the car, tucked a stray wisp of dark blond hair into the loose knot atop her head and adjusted the generous folds of her cool cotton gauze shift. In Washington she had been dressing for fall, but experiencing the island's balmy weather made her glad she'd chosen a more summery outfit that morning. As she reached through the open door for her green straw shoulder purse—the same pale sea shade as her dress—she heard a voice behind her.

"You shouldn't pull out into the road like that, with no warning. It's very dangerous. I almost plowed right into you. We could both have been hurt. Killed, even. Do you know what the statistical chances are that—"

Verna wheeled around. The driver of that Jag talked the way he drove—fast and furious. How dare he try to give her a lecture on statistics, she thought. She was the one who should be lecturing him—on safe driving habits. "If you hadn't been in such a hurry—" she began hotly.

"I guess you're right," he interrupted, to her surprise. "I tend to be in a hurry," he said with a shrug. "I have a lot to do." Then he smiled and thrust out his hand. "My name is Mel Hopkins."

As he shook her hand, he looked her over, forthrightly and carefully, from head to foot. Usually men looked no farther down than her chin. The scrutiny was extremely disarming. "I'm Verna Myers," she said, finding her voice and enough composure to look him in the eye.

She was no shorty—five-eight in her stockinged feet and more in the canvas wedgies she was wearing—but she had to lift her chin quite a bit to meet his dark-brown eyes. A bumper crop of dark-brown curls tumbled over his forehead. There were a few coils of silver in the curls, and she guessed he was in his early thirties, a few years older than herself. Still, his face was unlined and boyish with an open, even vulnerable, expression. His eyes, however, shone with keen intelligence and knowledge beyond his years.

"Verna," he repeated, rolling the name around on his tongue as if it were a sip of fine brandy. "Very unusual.

You must be one of a very small percentage of women to be called Verna." He hurried on with less assurance than he'd begun with. "There are probably more men called Verne than women called Verna, but I couldn't be sure of that until I looked up the figures. I've never known anyone called Verna before," he trailed off.

Few people had commented on her name in the past and none with statistical probabilities in mind. She didn't know quite what to say to him. He was an odd mixture of charm and awkwardness. She opted for brightness. "Well, I've never known anyone called Mel before. Except Mel Gibson. Unfortunately, he doesn't know me," she finished with a too loud laugh.

He responded to her joke with a curious look. "Who's Mel Gibson?"

She was taken aback. *I may not be up on much, but I do know a few of the hot actors.* "He's an Australian actor," she explained. "He was in *Beyond Thunderdome* and *Mad Max* and *Gallipoli* and *The Year of Living Dangerously* and *The River . . .*"

He gave her a puzzled look, as if she were naming the members of a rare species of poisonous lizard rather than popular films. "I don't get to the movies much."

"No, I guess you don't."

There was a short pause, and Mel Hopkins reached into the pocket of his short-sleeved plaid shirt. The chinos he wore with it were equally unprepossessing, Verna noted. He produced two cellophane-wrapped caramels and held them out in his open palm. "Want one? They're my last two."

Verna shook her head.

"Suit yourself." He twisted the paper from one and popped the candy into his mouth.

"Oh, what the heck," she said rashly and took the other caramel. It was sweet and sticky and satisfyingly chewy.

When they had both swallowed, they looked at each other and grinned guiltily. They were like kids who had shared an experimental cigarette behind the garage, bonded by their secret. The sweet taste in Verna's mouth turned suddenly sour, and she looked away from him. *This is exactly the sort of thing I came here to stop*, she thought angrily. "Thanks," she said curtly, and started to walk away. "I guess I'll be seeing you later."

"Wait a minute." He came after her. "I didn't force you to take that caramel, you know."

"No, you didn't," she said, relenting.

"I was just trying to be friendly."

"I know." If friendship was going to lead to temptation, however, she'd be better off without it while she was at the Last Resort. "But I didn't come here to make friends."

"Neither did I. But that doesn't mean I'm unalterably opposed to it. Or to other, um, forms of human relationships." He gave her another of those disconcerting head-to-toe looks.

She shifted uncomfortably and edged away. She didn't want that kind of interest from any man—much less Mel Hopkins—until she could look at herself in the mirror with impunity. She'd have to steer as clear as possible of this character, which might not be easy in such close quarters. "Guess I'd better go and register," she said as she turned and headed off.

"See you at lunch," he called after her.

Not if I have anything to do with it, she thought without looking back.

VERNA SIGNED IN at the desk and was directed to her accommodation in a cluster of small town houses a few minutes' walk from the main building. The houses were made of the same gray-toned wood as the main building with the same clean, modern lines. But they also had traditional Southern grace with their landscaped gardens and wide porches. There were two sturdy wooden rocking chairs on the well-shaded porch and large clay pots brimming with white and yellow chrysanthemums. She could see herself rocking in one of the chairs, resting after a long energetic day, sipping a cool drink, losing herself in one of the novels she loved but so rarely had time for.

The porch was to be shared with an upstairs neighbor, but she had the ground floor of the small house to herself. She let herself into the living room, restfully furnished in beiges and blues. The bedroom lay beyond, and through the connecting door she could see a sliding glass door that led onto a small patio containing a couple of lounge chairs. She went to it, slid the glass door open and stepped out. The view was gorgeous—over the dunes with their tall, waving grasses and down to the sea. She stood watching the waves crest and peak, feeling the cares and tensions of Washington recede, as if she'd piled them into a boat and they were being swept out to sea.

"Lovely, isn't it?" Verna turned at the sound of a soft female voice coming from the next patio. The woman she saw wore a flowing dress in a bold peacock blue that made her silver hair seem to shimmer in the bright daylight. The dress was striking but served only as a background—like the velvet in a jeweler's window—for the intricate silver-and-lapis necklace that reclined regally in the wide V of its neckline. When the woman came near, Verna caught the sweet scent of gardenia. "I'm Florence Hathaway," she said.

Verna introduced herself and shook the immaculately manicured hand Mrs. Hathaway extended. At least she assumed it was Mrs. from the wide carved silver band that covered most of the space between the second joint and knuckle of the ring finger of her left hand. "I don't mean to gawk, but I can hardly keep my eyes off your stunning necklace, Mrs. Hathaway."

"Florence, please. There's no need for neighbors to be so formal. And thank you. It's my own design," she added modestly. "I have a small shop in Savannah."

The women exchanged a few more pleasantries, then Verna excused herself to unpack and freshen up. Her bedroom was furnished with a handsome cherry suite and decorated with breezy flowered chintz drapes and a spread in subtle pinks and greens. An easy chair and ottoman were covered with a complementary fabric. There was a large closet and a tiny kitchenette with a sink. A midget refrigerator and a hot plate, as well as a supply of mineral water and a variety of herbal teas. She completed her tour by inspecting the bath, which had moss-green fixtures and plenty of clean fluffy towels.

From the door of the bath she surveyed the bedroom. Everything was very much to her liking. The resort, carefully planned to provide a restful, relaxing atmosphere, was working its magic on her already. Too bad, she thought, they couldn't extend that same control to their clients. She wasn't going to let her unsettling encounter with Mel Hopkins spoil her enjoyment or lessen her achievements during the month-long stay, however. She had worked too hard to arrange such a long leave and pinched too many pennies for that.

Verna finished unpacking just in time to get to the introductory luncheon session. Florence Hathaway was stepping down from her porch as Verna was leaving, so the two women walked to the main building together, along a path well shaded with live oaks and pines and palmetto palms.

The lounge where they had been asked to gather before lunch was furnished with comfortable rattan sofas and chairs, their cushions covered in a cheerful red-flowered print. There was a small bar where a young woman glowing with health served iced herbal tea and mineral water. People were gathered in small knots, and the snatches of conversation Verna overheard as she and Florence made their way to the bar were those of strangers getting acquainted—where do you come from? what do you do?—the sort of chatter that allows people to make connections where none existed before.

She suspected, however, that no one had broached the one subject that made an immediate and undeniable connection between them all. She and Florence had skirted it. Mel Hopkins had alluded to it with his caramels, but as yet no one had met the subject head-on. Verna herself had not told anyone her reason for taking this expensive vacation. But as she sipped her iced mint tea and looked around the room, the one thing all these people had in common was only too evident.

They were all fat.

Never mind the euphemisms, Verna thought. *Forget overweight, full figured, imposing, plump, chubby, chunky, hefty, stocky, stout or "a bit broad in the beams." Everyone here, including me, is fat.*

It felt good to face up to it, if only to herself. And better still to realize that not only she, but the other eleven registrants in the room, as well, were there to do something about it.

"Do you think anyone would want to take bets on the collective weight in the room, and on how much we're going to lose? I brought a PC, you know, a personal computer. I could work out a program, and we could have a pool every day, kind of like pari-mutuel betting at the racetrack."

Mel Hopkins was rattling away at her like a clacking Teletype machine, starting up without so much as a "hello" or "how are you." "I don't know if that would be quite in keeping with the spirit of the place," she said in what she hoped was a discouraging tone.

"Don't get the wrong idea," he put in quickly. "It's not the gambling I like. I couldn't care less about that. It's the numbers. I love to see how they line up and fall down, and I love to write programs. That's what I do, you see. Write computer programs. I have a company. It's called Peony Enterprises. I wrote Peony. You may have heard of it. It's a spreadsheet. The whole country's using it, to judge from our sales figures. What do you do?"

If Mel Hopkins ate as fast and as much as he talked, she could see why he'd ended up here at the Last Resort. She knew that if he'd invented Peony, however, his brain cells couldn't be too flabby. Senator Carlsen's accounting staff used the program and raved about it. She realized he was looking at her eagerly and remembered he'd asked her a question. "I work on Capitol Hill," she answered flatly, not betraying the interest he had aroused.

Mel Hopkins was not deterred by her tone. "That must be interesting. What exactly do you do? Do you work for a congressman? Congressperson?" he amended quickly. "I wouldn't want you to think I assume all members of Congress are men."

In spite of herself, Verna warmed to him a little. Too few men were sensitive to that kind of assumption, and fewer still would admit to it. "I work for a senator," she said, "Agatha Carlsen of Iowa."

"I worked for someone once who was running for office, doing statistical analysis of opinion polls, voting projections, that sort of thing. Now *there* were some fascinating numbers . . ." His voice trailed off. "I seem to turn every conversation back to numbers, don't I? That's one of the reasons I've come here. Not just to drop a few pounds, but to meet people who do more than shift numbers around all day. I can't understand it, but not everyone finds it as endlessly fascinating as I do."

"Everyone has that trouble when they're passionate about something. I see my friends' eyes glaze over all the time when I get into a blow-by-blow account of a particularly convoluted political wrangle. Every twist and turn is interesting to me, but even a lot of people from the Hill get bored quickly."

He took a step closer. "You can try out your stories on me anytime. I won't be bored. I love convolutions."

He turned a winsome smile on her, open and frankly inviting. She was undeniably flattered by his attention but found the situation ironic nonetheless. For months she'd been sitting on the edge of her chair, hoping and praying that Jim Byram would notice her. Now, when she least wanted male attention, it had come to her.

Although from a rather unlikely source. She doubted there was a single suave bone in Mel Hopkins's amply padded body. Still, there was something appealing in his unsophistication. So many of the men she knew in Washington—Jim Byram excepted, of course—were hard-edged and calculating. It was refreshing, she decided, to meet a man who confined his manipulations to numbers. What harm could there be in a friendship with him? She would have to be careful not to be too friendly, though. She wouldn't want to give him the wrong impression.

She turned back to him, prepared with an open but casual smile. She was totally unprepared, however, for the way his deep brown eyes lit up when she looked up at him. Nor did she expect—or welcome—the jolting thump in her chest that came as a response to the light in his eyes.

Verna excused herself hurriedly and rushed to the bar for a refill of iced mint tea. *What have I done?* she asked herself angrily. *I've come here to lose weight, not to start a romance.* From the corner of her eye she saw that Mel was standing where she'd left him, looking bewil-

dered. She took a long pull on her tea, feeling rather
bewildered herself. Why was she making such a big deal
about a couple of looks that passed between her and a
stranger? Her job required a cool and logical head, and
ninety-nine percent of the time that's exactly what she
had. Why was she feeling so flustered now?

"Everyone seems very friendly, don't they?"

She looked up to see that Florence Hathaway was
standing beside her. "Yes, very," she answered politely,
thinking that some of her fellow guests were a bit too
friendly.

"I've met so many interesting people. This is going
to be more fun than I thought. Oh, look, Verna, over
there."

Verna and Florence were not the only people who had
turned their attention to the door. Nearly everyone was
gawking at the gray-haired man who had just entered
the room. "That must be Dr. Clifford, the director,"
Florence gushed. "He's even more handsome than his
picture," she said in a fluttery voice. "Don't you just
love the way his tan sets off his hair? It's like gold
against silver." She giggled girlishly. "Trust me to com-
pare a handsome man to precious metals."

The sight of the man didn't send Verna into the same
paroxysms of delight as her older companion. She
could not deny, however, that the director exuded an
aura of energy and electricity. At the same time he
seemed totally relaxed. Despite the lack of fanfare or
announcement of his arrival, the cocktail-party chatter died down and an air of anticipation settled over the
room.

Dr. Clifford moved unhurriedly among the small knots of people, greeting his clients and shaking hands. When he had spoken to everyone personally, he addressed the gathering. "Make yourselves comfortable, ladies and gentlemen. I have a few brief remarks, and then we'll go in to lunch." He waited until everyone had settled on sofas and chairs and then nimbly hopped onto a bar stool.

A pang of envy shot through Verna as she watched his lithe movements. She hadn't been able to move that easily since she was a teenager, and George Clifford had to be at least twice her age. *But I will be able to,* she vowed. This time she was determined to get slim and trim and stay that way. So slim and trim that she might even take up early-morning running in Rock Creek Park. The way to Jim Byram's heart could well be through his feet. Heaven knew his stomach was not on the route.

"The first thing I'd like to say is that after the next four weeks I never want to see any of you again." Dr. Clifford paused as a nervous titter spread through the room. "I mean that," he continued. "I named this place the Last Resort for two very good reasons. I know that most of you—all of you—have been on and off diets for many years. If they'd worked, you wouldn't be here. Coming here is the last resort for many of you. And I want it to stay that way. The second reason I chose the name is that I want you all to see that we have a sense of humor about what we're doing here. We'd like you to have one, too. The changes you'll be making in your eating and exercise habits may be hard to get used to at first, but I think the ability to find the light side of things will help you as much, and possibly more, than the determination and willpower I know you've brought with you."

Verna felt herself loosen up as she listened to Dr. Clifford's soothing voice. She saw that her fellow guests were starting to enjoy themselves, too. She hadn't known quite what to expect from the Last Resort and had imagined everything from military boot camp to a sybaritic spa. The actual experience, she realized, would lie somewhere between the two extremes. Life for the next four weeks would be disciplined but not unduly rigorous, comfortable but not overly pampered.

As Dr. Clifford explained the schedule of meals and activities, Verna realized she was starting to feel very hungry. "There will be two exercise periods each day— one in the morning and one in the afternoon. We also expect everyone to walk for half an hour after breakfast and lunch. You may take a walk after dinner, as well, but it's not required. Nevertheless, most guests do after the first week or so, when they've become accustomed to regular vigorous exercise. Don't be alarmed by the amount of physical exercise. The classes will be easy to start with and build as your stamina increases. Remember, your personal physicians have given you the go-ahead for this program, and I'm on call twenty-four hours a day if you need me."

Verna tried to concentrate on what Dr. Clifford was saying, but the thought of all that exercise made her mind stray to the hearty Southern-style breakfast she'd had in Charleston. Her hotel had offered a groaning buffet table, always a hard temptation to resist. She'd started off virtuously with a bowl of fresh fruit. But when she went back to the buffet, she'd filled her plate with flaky biscuits, spicy sausage patties, fluffy scrambled eggs and steaming hominy grits smothered in melted butter. Except for the grits, the breakfast reminded her of the farmhouse fare she grew up on in Iowa. Whenever she had something challenging to face, she started the day with a meal like that. It gave her courage. It also gave her megadoses of fat and cholesterol. Like many people who struggled with their weight, she had read widely and was knowledgeable about many issues of health and weight control. *That's what I'm here to discover,* she thought wryly. *A formula for courage without cholesterol.* She smiled to herself and turned her full attention back to Dr. Clifford.

"Before we go in to lunch," he was saying, "I'd like to introduce the two people who will be working most closely with you."

He motioned to a man and a woman standing by the door. The man was about six feet tall, with sunbleached blond hair and a physique that any man would have made a pact with the devil to have. He wore form-fitting jeans, a cerulean polo shirt that matched his eyes and a dazzling smile. The woman standing next to him was just as much a knockout. Her rich copper hair was pulled back from her perky features and tumbled over her strong, lean shoulders. Her sunny smile almost eclipsed the bright splotches of color in her two-piece cotton dress.

"This is Don Miller and Carrie Donohue. They'll be monitoring your individual exercise programs and leading the group seminars. I think you'll find them very sympathetic and understanding, not only because they know and love their work, but because they are both graduates of the Last Resort."

A collective gasp, almost in unison, filled the room. Here were two people looking the way everyone in the world—except perhaps Robert Redford and Daryl Hannah—wanted to look, and they had once been as overweight and out of shape as the people they would be supervising. It was almost too much to take in.

"Does that mean," Mel Hopkins called out, "that I'll look like Don this time next month?"

"Not unless you dye your hair blond," Don Miller quipped in response.

Everyone in the room laughed, including Verna. She found the thought of Mel Hopkins being transformed into a superstud especially amusing. *He's got a long way to go*, she thought, *and it will take more than a month and a bottle of hair bleach.*

Dr. Clifford rose and started toward the dining room. "If you'll follow me, ladies and gentlemen, please. There are no assigned places in the dining room, so please sit where you like."

Oh, no, Verna said to herself. *He'll undoubtedly try to sit at my table.* Luckily she and Florence were among the farthest from the door to the dining room, and Mel was among the nearest. If she could hold back for a moment or two, perhaps the table where he sat would be filled. She almost laughed aloud at the thought of trying to be the last one in to a meal. Usually she couldn't wait to get to the table.

Her strategy worked. There were two seats left at the table where Carrie Donohue was sitting and she and Florence slid into them. The dining room was as pleasant as all the rooms at the resort. Half a dozen round tables were covered with pale apricot linen cloths. The tables were set with bisque-colored china and shell-motif flatware. There was a small vase of fresh flowers on each table. From her seat Verna had a view of the ocean through a large picture window.

As she unfolded her napkin, she was conscious of being nervous, as overweight people often are when they eat with strangers. She took a sip of ice water from her glass and glanced around the table surreptitiously. The others—except for Carrie—seemed to be concerned about something, too, and Verna had a hunch that their thinking was moving along lines similar to hers.

Lunch turned out to be surprisingly delicious. She was expecting two strawberries and a tablespoon of cottage cheese, artfully arranged on a single lettuce leaf, but the meal was much more substantial and satisfying. There was a small cup of clear broth dotted with still crunchy vegetables, followed by broiled salmon garnished with fresh dill, a small baked potato and a bowl of crisp greens with creamy yogurt dressing. If Verna had chosen the meal herself, the soup would have been full of cream and butter, the salmon steak at least three times as large. She'd have had sour cream and chives on the potato and a large dollop of blue-cheese dressing on the salad. Because the portions were what her mother would derisively have described as dainty, she ate slowly, chewing each bite carefully. To her surprise she found she was full when the waitress cleared away her empty plate. Ordinarily she would have craved a rich sticky desert, but she found she was quite happy with the stemmed glass of chilled red-and-green grapes that was placed in front of her.

Perhaps it was the beautiful, restful setting, or that no one else in the room was eating anything fattening, or the conversation and camaraderie, but Verna enjoyed her meal more than she'd enjoyed any meal she'd eaten in a long while. She sat back contentedly and sipped the delicious coffee the waitress poured from a steaming glass pot.

Dr. Clifford stood and clinked a spoon lightly against his water glass. "We'll adjourn for our post-lunch walk now. The beach, of course, is excellent for walking." Verna didn't have to think long to remember where she'd heard that before. *Good for what ails you*, Jim had said.

"Or if you prefer," Dr. Clifford was saying, "there are paths through the woods. You'll see the signs about two hundred yards to the right of the entrance to the lounge. At two-thirty your first seminar with Don and Carrie will start. For the seminars, only, we've divided you into two groups." He read out the assignments and the location of each meeting. Don's group was to meet in Conference Room A, Carrie's in Conference Room B. The six people in Don Miller's group didn't include her or Mel Hopkins, she noted with some annoyance. That meant it would be even harder to avoid being thrown into contact with him. As a consolation, however, Florence Hathaway would also be in her group. During the meal Verna had found herself liking the gracious woman more and more.

"I'll be meeting with everyone," Dr. Clifford continued, "at five o'clock in Conference Room A. Dinner will be served at six-thirty. I look forward to seeing you all then." Chairs had started to scrape against the hardwood floors when he called for their attention once again. "One more thing, ladies and gentlemen. You may have noticed that we serve no caffeinic beverages. Caffeine is a substance its users frequently crave, and we want to eliminate all your food cravings. There's also a strong association between taking caffeine and eating sweets, and we want to break that, too. Those of you who are used to drinking tea or coffee or colas may find that you have a headache later in the afternoon. Don't be alarmed. It's a perfectly normal reaction and should go away within twenty-four hours."

Verna turned to Florence in surprise. "You mean that wasn't real coffee we were drinking? I always thought decaffeinated coffee had to taste like dishwater."

"I fancy myself a rather good judge of coffees," Florence replied, "and all I missed was that bit of chicory I usually add to my special blend." They rose and started toward the door. "Shall we walk together, Verna? What would you prefer? The beach or the footpath through the woods?"

"Beach," Verna declared without hesitation. "I'm from Iowa and I still get excited when I see the ocean. Let's leave our shoes on the porch. I love to squiggle my toes in the sand."

"Good choice," Florence said. She leaned close to Verna and lowered her voice. "We'll have to go back to my room for a minute first, though. I'm still old-fashioned enough to be wearing hose."

"When it's this warm, I'm only old-fashioned on workdays," Verna confided as they walked to Florence's door. "I can't stand the way panty hose get bunched up around my waist. So on weekends and vacations I give them up if I can."

"Panty hose are a sheer delight, my dear, compared to the girdles and garter belts of yesteryear. My heavens, it was like wearing a suit of armor under your clothes. And in our Southern heat! Even when I was a young slip of a thing, without an excess ounce, I wore all that paraphernalia. Everyone did. No 'lady' would have dreamed of doing otherwise." She laughed ruefully. "You're probably too young to remember all that."

"I have heard my mother and aunts talk about it. I must admit it doesn't sound like a lot of fun."

They reached Florence's door, and Verna waited on the porch until Florence came out carrying a pair of white thongs which she left on the porch beside Verna's canvas wedgies. A narrow boardwalk beside the town houses passed between the dunes and down to the beach. They walked on the hard-packed sand above the waterline but once or twice wet their toes in the cooling surf for respite from the hot sun. They'd been walking for more than ten minutes when Verna said, "We'd better start back if we want to rinse our feet off before the seminar."

Florence glanced at her watch. "Have we been walking that long? It seems like we just started. Walking is something no one thinks about doing anymore.

Everyone's either driving or jogging. I'd forgotten how pleasant it is."

"It is that," Verna agreed. Although she'd taken an occasional walk in Rock Creek Park or along the Mall, there simply didn't seem to be time in her busy life for such simple pleasures. "We walked everywhere as kids. Or rode our bikes. Now that's something I haven't done in a long time, either. I understand there are bikes available for our use. Shall we go for a ride sometime?"

"We can try," Florence said with a laugh. "I'm not sure I remember how."

"It's something you're never supposed to forget."

"We'll see about that. But I'm game. I'll try anything once. Besides, if I fall off, I've got enough padding to cushion the fall."

"Now you do. But not for long. Right?"

"Right!"

Verna and Florence grinned at each other like soldiers about to vanquish a common enemy, then marched quickly and determinedly back to the resort.

2

CONFERENCE ROOM B HAD a view of woods, not sea. It also had a blackboard, a tripod for charts and a movie screen that could be pulled down when needed. Six chairs had been arranged in a semicircle at the front of the room; a seventh faced the semicircle. Carrie Donohue stood at the door and greeted each of her charges for the two-thirty seminar. Verna and Florence, delayed by foot rinsing, were the last to file in. As she stepped into the room, Mel Hopkins waved at her as if he were trying to flag her down in a crowded ballpark. "Over here, Verna," he called from the center of the circle. "I saved you a seat."

No one's saved me a seat since the high-school cafeteria, she thought, trying not to laugh. But he had a kind of natural friskiness, an irrepressible enthusiasm, that compelled the corners of her mouth to turn up. She glanced at Florence, who was also smiling. The women exchanged an amused shrug as Verna slid into the seat beside Mel.

"So," he said heartily, "how do you like the torture so far?"

"Torture? That's not how I'd describe it. I'm enjoying myself a great deal."

"Hah! Wait until tomorrow when they make us exercise. I can manage walking. I've been doing that since

I was a baby. But I'm such a klutz at everything else. The chance that I'll make a fool of myself is statistically very good. Excellent, in fact. Nobody could beat those odds, even me."

Verna was surprised by the good humor with which he spoke. Most people who thought they were about to make fools of themselves neither advertised the fact nor were cheerful about it. "I'm not much good at sports or exercise, either," she assured him. "Come to think of it, I don't suppose any of us are very good at sports—or we wouldn't be in the shape we're in."

"You've got a point there. I bet it would be fun to do a study of the correlation between being overweight and levels of physical coordination. I bet those numbers would be real interesting."

Verna couldn't decide if he were serious or not and gave a tentative chuckle. The odd look he gave her told her he hadn't been joking. *This guy is definitely one of a kind,* she thought.

Carrie Donohue had closed the door to the conference room and placed a blown-up photograph of an obese middle-aged woman on the tripod. Verna had always seen the thirty-five pounds she needed to lose as an insurmountable obstacle, but the woman in the photo was encased in four times that much excess fat. No one in the room was close to needing that kind of weight reduction.

"Trying to make us feel better, Carrie?" Mel asked brashly.

"In a way," Carrie replied. "Do any of you recognize the person in this photograph?"

"Sophia Loren on a bad day?" Mel shot back.

Verna laughed along with the rest of the group but privately wondered how Mel had managed to hear of Sophia Loren. Unless he'd been putting her on before about Mel Gibson. Carrie's answer, however, stopped all thoughts of Mel Hopkin's knowledge of film stars.

"Good guess, but wrong," Carrie said. It's me."

There was stunned silence in the room.

"That can't be you, honey," Florence said after a moment. "That person has to be at least forty years old."

"That picture was taken just after my high-school graduation," Carrie told the still disbelieving group. "I was eighteen years old. I weighed almost two hundred fifty pounds, more than twice what I weigh today."

Verna peered at the photograph. By looking very closely she could discern the outline of Carrie's features in the rounded cheeks and double chin. "How in the world did you lose all that weight? And keep it off?"

"For a graduation present my parents sent me to Dr. Clifford. My month here gave me a good start. It took me more than a year to lose the rest of the weight, but I was determined and I did it. Once I'd done it, I realized I wanted to work with people who were fighting the same battles that I had won, so I studied nutrition and physical education in college. Then I went on for a master's degree in clinical psychology. I'd kept in touch with Dr. Clifford while I was in school, and he offered me a job after graduation. I've been here for two years now."

Verna was highly inspired by Carrie's story. Her thirty-five unwanted pounds didn't seem nearly so unshakable now.

"I always start off the first seminar with this picture," Carrie told the group. "You know the old saying about not understanding a person's problems until you've walked a mile in his moccasins. I had some pretty big mocccasins—as you can see." She removed the photo from the tripod and replaced it with a hand-lettered poster. "We take a two-pronged approach to weight loss here." She pointed to the column on the left of the poster. "On the one side we have behavior modification: teaching you to choose the foods and exercise routines that will maximize your health and energy level and minimize your weight." She moved her hand to the column on the right side. "We also want you to understand why you consistently choose foods that are not good for you, why you eat when you're not hungry, why you eat more than you really want, why you don't get enough exercise."

Carrie sat down in the chair that faced the group. "What we're going to do now is probably the hardest thing you'll face in the next four weeks—harder than the discouragement you'll feel, the impatience, the food cravings. I would like each of you to tell the group why you're here, how you came to have a weight problem and what you hope to do about it here." No one in the group looked at anyone else, but Verna could feel the uneasiness in herself and her fellow classmates.

"I know this won't be easy," Carrie went on, "but if you can get over this rise, everything else will be downhill. Unless I have any volunteers to start, I'll pick a name out of a hat." There were—understandably—no takers, and she reached into a small cardboard box that she'd obviously prepared for just such a case and took out a slip of paper. "Verna Myers," she read. Smiling encouragingly at Verna, she said, "You get to get it over with first."

Verna had often thought about the reasons for her weight problem, but she'd never been called on to articulate them. In her job she was often called upon to make impromptu speeches, so she wasn't nervous about speaking in front of a group. The things she talked about, however, were the farm bill, gun control, tax revision—never herself. She was somewhat apprehensive about addressing a group of strangers on so intimate a topic. She hesitated for a moment, collecting her thoughts and reminding herself that everyone else in the room was in the same boat as she was.

"I grew up on a farm in Iowa," she began in a low, controlled voice. "There was always plenty of hearty food to match hearty appetites. Like all my brothers and sisters, I had my share of chores to do and I did them, but when they had a chance, they'd be off playing with the dogs or fishing or hiking. Every chance I got, I'd sit under a tree to read. I didn't need as much food as they did, but I ate just as much, so I've always been overweight. Only I didn't really notice it until I was a teenager. Since then I've been losing weight and gaining it right back.

"It's funny. My family has been very supportive of me in many respects, but they never gave me much help with my diets. I was the only one of seven children to leave the farm, to become anything other than a farmer or farmer's wife. I don't lift anything heavier than a book of law abstracts in my job, but I still eat as if I were on the farm. I guess it's my way of saying I'm still a part of the family."

The room had become quite still and the sound of her own voice reverberated in her ears. The importance of her last sentence also echoed inside her. She'd never thought of eating as a way of staying close to her family, but there it was, the crux of the matter, as plain as day. "That's all," she said quickly. She didn't want to have to say anymore until she'd had a chance to mull over her revelation in private.

Carrie didn't press her. "Thank you very much, Verna." She took a piece of chalk and wrote on the blackboard: Loyalty. "If you think you're being disloyal to family or friends by refusing food, then of course you're going to eat more than you really need or want. We can see from Verna's story how strong a motivation it is. Let's go on. Who wants to go next?"

"Me," Mel volunteered.

"Take it away," Carrie invited.

Mel jumped in without hesitation. "I like to be world-class in everything I do. I'm brilliant at three things: computers, statistics and food. So that's just about all I do. I graduated from high school when I was twelve and had a PhD by the time I was eighteen, so I never played sports or games or had hobbies like other kids. I studied and I ate. Now I work and eat. I know I'm missing a lot. I'd like to do more, to be more a part of the world. I'm trying, but I still hesitate to do anything if I can't do it brilliantly. Therefore, I'd like to know what it's like to be merely successful—not necessarily brilliant—at something. Losing weight seems the logical place to start."

Verna would have been very skeptical of most people who labeled themselves as brilliant, but with Mel it was merely a statement of fact. He wasn't trying to impress people or intimidate them. His assessment and conclusions were as rational as a mathematical equation. He might be somewhat gauche, but his clearheaded assessments were a welcome change from the preening and self-satisfaction of many of the men she knew in Washington. Thinking of DC naturally led her to the subject of Jim Byram. He didn't preen, but now that she thought about it, she could see a distinct tendency toward self-righteousness. And he'd never have allowed himself to appear so vulnerable, she thought. Yet Mel had no trouble letting his defenses down. *What am I doing?!?* she yelled at herself. *Comparing Jim to Mel Hopkins?* Maybe they put brain suppressants in the water here. She couldn't think of any other explanation.

Verna turned her attention back to Carrie, who had written on the blackboard: Narrow Life Focus. "I hear a lot of people say they eat out of boredom, but that isn't the case with you, Mel. We'll have to work on redirecting your considerable energy."

Florence Hathaway took the floor next and talked about eating to allay all sorts of anxieties—the success of her business, holding on to her husband when so many of her friends' husbands were leaving them for younger, slimmer women, watching her children leave home and get along without her. Verna was struck by the disparity in the way Florence described herself and how self-assured she had seemed when they met. If she was hiding that many insecurities all the time, no wonder she sought solace in food.

Another woman spoke about her lack of willpower, her inability to say no to anything or anyone, especially where food was concerned. A busy executive complained about his hectic schedule and the constant rounds of business entertaining that made it impossible to stick to a sensible diet and exercise routine. The last speaker timidly explained how food had become her best friend after her husband died.

Two hours passed so quickly that Verna was truly surprised when Carrie said they would have to stop. They had thirty minutes before Dr. Clifford's introductory lecture to all the participants, which would be followed by the evening meal. Carrie suggested a short leg-stretching walk before the start of the next session. "You'd better get used to being on the go," she counseled. "There won't be this much sitting in one day for the next four weeks. I can promise you that."

The group rose and started for the door. As they passed her, Carrie had a word of encouragement for everyone. Her enthusiasm and concern were so genuine that Verna felt she was really going to be able to do it this time—lose those pounds and keep them off.

She left the room imagining a trim, svelte Verna in a high-fashion designer suit, hurrying along the corridors of the Capitol Building, confident, proud, bursting with energy, the type of woman who could be elected to follow in Agatha Carlsen's footsteps, the type of woman Jim Byram had been looking for all his life.

Her reverie was interrupted by a voice close to her ear. "Some bunch of true confessions, eh?" Mel asked in what seemed to her a needlessly disparaging tone.

"I happen to like the truth," she answered haughtily, still feeling the sense of high purpose her imaginary trip down the legislative halls had engendered. As a member of Congress it would be her job to defend the truth, to protect it from the political necessities that tarnished it all too often.

"I've got nothing against it myself," Mel answered, feeling a bit confused by her. Verna Myers was one of the prettiest women he'd ever seen, but her mood shifted more easily than desert sand. He knew he didn't have much of an account in the cool-and-smooth bank, but he also knew he wasn't totally undesirable. Now that he was rich and a little bit famous, he'd even had a couple of women chasing him. But he hadn't been attracted to them the way he was to Verna. Getting her to like him was just like balancing an equation, he decided. All he had to do was find the right formula. He'd found plenty of those before. It ought to be a piece of cake. Or maybe a stick of celery, now that cake was no longer a part of his life.

"Want to stretch our legs together?" He tried to sound nonchalant when he asked but could have kicked himself when his voice cracked like a teenager's.

For a moment Verna was tempted to say yes. A male voice hadn't cracked in her presence since she was twelve. In a way it was rather endearing. Knowing what she now knew about him it was hard to say no, but she reminded herself that she'd come here to get things straightened out for herself. That had to be her first priority. She turned him down politely but firmly. "Thanks, but I've got a few things I'd like to think about on my own right now." He looked at her like a Saint Bernard with no one to rescue, so disappointed that she almost changed her mind. "Another time, maybe," she suggested.

Mel's face lit up like a Christmas tree. "How about after dinner?"

"How about tomorrow?" Verna countered gently.

The tree lights went out as if they'd been connected to an overloaded circuit. "Okay," he agreed reluctantly and walked away.

Oh dear, Verna thought with dismay. *I didn't mean to hurt his feelings. But he seems to be so sensitive.* She set off at a brisk pace, trying to use each step to whisk her mind clear of Mel Hopkins. She wanted to brush her thoughts into a neat pile, but every few steps the pile toppled. Mel continued to sweep into her mind like a warm and insistent summer breeze.

3

THE NEXT MORNING Verna woke up feeling ravenously hungry. Her first thought was of a plate of bacon and eggs accompanied by a stack of hot buttered toast. Then she remembered where she was. Bacon and eggs and butter were full of fat and cholesterol. She wouldn't be getting any such breakfast here at the Last Resort. And just as well, she told herself firmly.

She looked at the clock and realized that breakfast would not be served for more than an hour. She decided to make herself a cup of herbal tea in her tiny kitchenette and then go for a walk on the beach. That not only would take her mind off her rumbling tummy, but it would be good for her, too. She rose and dressed in ice-blue sweatpants and a lavender sweatshirt, drank her tea and headed for the beach.

It was utterly quiet, except for the occasional call of the gulls as they dived for their morning fish. Verna watched them as she walked, keeping up the steady rhythm Dr. Clifford had advised in his lecture the evening before. Soon her heart rate rose and the blood pumped steadily through her body. She breathed more deeply, filling her lungs with the invigorating salt air. All thoughts of bacon and eggs vanished. She enjoyed the cool of the morning, the gentle warmth of the early-morning sun on her face and her own company.

When she returned to her apartment, she had just enough time to freshen up and get to the dining room for breakfast. She knocked on Florence's door on her way and they walked to the dining room together.

Florence wore a warm-up suit of white jersey piped with vivid pink. She looked down at her outfit self-consciously as she stepped out the door. "This is the first time in years I haven't worn a dress shaped like a tent. I could hardly feel more embarrassed if I were naked." She sighed and then laughed. "Of course, I *could*. I came here in October because I thought the weather would be cool enough for sweat suits. I don't think I could handle being seen in shorts. It'll take me awhile to get used to this."

"I'm finding it rather liberating," Verna said, thinking of the dark figure-hiding suits she wore to work. "Not having to dress to hide your flaws."

"Yes," Florence began doubtfully. Then a gleam appeared in her eye. "I suppose there's some merit in 'letting it all hang out.'"

"You could put it that way," Verna replied with a chuckle.

Breakfast consisted of a bowl of fresh fruit topped with low-fat yogurt, a freshly baked whole-grain muffin and hot beverages. The muffin was delicious and Verna could happily have eaten another, but she knew that seconds wouldn't be served. So she made the treat last. She savored every tiny morsel, leaving not even a crumb on the plate.

After the meal Carrie appeared and reminded the group that the first class of the day would convene after the required half-hour walk. *But I've just done that,*

Verna said to herself. She'd forgotten earlier that she would be required to march off after breakfast. *Well, it certainly can't hurt my thighs,* she told herself as she left the dining room. As she'd already walked on the beach, she convinced Florence to try the path through the woods.

At the end of the thirty-minute walk Verna's energy was flagging. It was only nine-thirty, but she was already tired and hot. *Where's your old farm stamina?* she chided herself. As she trudged into the classroom, she decided she must have left it down on the farm.

The first class of the day was yoga. The instructor, a young woman with a fantastically lithe, elastic body, introduced herself as Sallie Wilmont and told them she'd also be teaching them aerobic dancing. In the shimmery bodysuit that fitted her like a second skin she looked to Verna like an electric blue rubber band. Sallie proceeded to lead the class through a series of maneuvers that would have taxed the flexibility of an unbaked pretzel. To Verna they didn't seem humanly possible, but there was Sallie, living proof that the yoga postures could be performed.

Sallie instructed the class often to stretch only as far as they could without pushing or straining. For most of them, Verna included, that was not very far at all. With every other sentence she reminded them to breathe deeply into the abdomen, letting it expand on the inhalation and deflate on the exhalation, as she had demonstrated at the start of the hour.

Verna's body was so unused to this kind of activity that sometimes she couldn't locate the muscles Sallie wanted to stretch. She got through the first half-dozen moves, often bewildered but able to make somewhat plausible imitations of the teacher. When they got to the one Sallie called the half-spinal twist, however, Verna was indeed twisted, but in a way that did not remotely resemble the posture Sallie had demonstrated. Despite the careful instructions, she couldn't figure out which way to twist or which arm to press against the bent knee that was crossed over her straight leg.

Sallie, who moved through the room giving individual help to those who needed it most, noticed her confusion and came to help her. Gently she positioned Verna's arms and legs and head and even pointed out with light pressure of her fingers the exact muscles that were meant to benefit from the exercise. Finally Verna was able to make the correct twisting movement, looking over her right shoulder and pressing against her bent right leg with her left arm. She closed her eyes and concentrated on her breathing. As she did, she felt her body start to relax into the posture. *So that's how it's supposed to work*, she thought, pleased to know she was beginning to have an inkling of the benefits and joys of the strange new discipline.

Next Sallie asked them to lie on their backs with their arms at their sides. "This is called the corpse pose. Through the following exercise we will induce a state of deep relaxation." She talked them through the long sequence, instructing them to tense and then relax each part of the body in turn, coaching them to feel relaxation spreading from toes to head.

Verna was so tired from the morning's unaccustomed exercise that she drifted far, far away under Sallie's soothing voice. Even as she followed the instruction to return to a normal state of consciousness, she was aware that part of her mind wanted to remain in that other pleasant place she'd discovered during the exercise. Nevertheless, she coaxed herself to sit up slowly. As she took a final deep breath, she realized she was feeling refreshed and very, very calm.

"Open your eyes and look around the room to reorient yourself," Sallie advised.

As Verna turned to look behind her, she met Mel Hopkins's eyes. He smiled lazily at her, and Verna, full of peacefulness and good will, grinned back at him. After lunch, she decided, she'd ask him to take that walk she'd promised him yesterday.

There was a brief break for beverages, and then the group split up for a session with either Carrie or Don. In the group there was a freewheeling discussion on the stake each participant had in remaining overweight. A group dynamic was beginning to develop that Carrie fostered and guided expertly.

Lunch, which Verna welcomed the way a shipwrecked sailor welcomes a rescue vessel, had a Middle Eastern flavor. There was a small scoop of humus— spicy chick-pea paste—served with salad and a whole wheat pita pocket. Dessert was a frozen banana sprinkled with lemon juice and zesty grated lemon peel. Despite portions that still seemed minuscule to Verna, the meal was surprisingly satisfying. She left the table feeling well fed and full.

She hadn't noticed Mel leave the dining room, but when she went to look for him, he was gone. She stepped outside and looked both ways down the path, but there was no sight of him. *Strange*, she thought. *I expected him to be bugging me about that walk. Count your blessings*, she advised herself resolutely and started off on her own. She had only gone a few steps when Carl Hadley, the business executive in her group, caught up with her and suggested that they walk together. She was glad of the company as she and Carl headed for the beach.

MEL HAD PURPOSELY sneaked out of the dining room so that he wouldn't have to meet Verna. He waited around a corner where he had a view of the dining-room door to see which way Verna went. When he saw her head toward the beach with Carl, he turned off in the other direction for his walk.

He had every intention of taking her up on her offer, but he wanted to save that pleasure for after dinner. He'd found the previous evening long and tedious. After dinner, such as it was, he'd gone back to his room. But he had nothing to do there. He'd put the television on, tried to watch it for a while, but found all the offerings mindless and boring. Then he set up his PC and fooled around with some calculations, trying to work out a few bugs in a new program he was developing, but his heart wasn't in it. This was supposed to be a vacation. He was supposed to do something besides work in his free time.

Jack, his business partner, had been right. He should have brought his banjo. Krynicki played the fiddle in a bluegrass band in his spare time and had encouraged Mel to take up the banjo. He'd made some progress in the past six months but had refused to take his instrument along to the Last Resort. People might hear him practicing there, and he wasn't good enough for that yet. Now, though, he longed for the comfort he found in working out the complex fingering and matching it to the strumming. But he'd been too stubborn, too worried that he wasn't the world's greatest banjo player, to listen to Jack.

Instead, he spent the rest of the evening reading in German a book on a new computer language that had been developed in Germany, but couldn't keep his mind on it. Once he started a technical treatise, he was usually absorbed in it immediately. The only reason he ever put something aside was if he already knew what the author was writing about. But last night he couldn't have cared less about computer languages.

He only wanted to think about Verna. It was all he could do to keep her out of his head for twenty minutes. Lightning had struck. He knew exactly how small the statistical probability of that was, but he still couldn't help thinking of how he'd felt the day before when he first saw her face. *Why me, why her, why now?* he kept asking himself. The questions absorbed him for the full half-hour of his walk.

VERNA COULDN'T HELP but notice that Mel was eyeing her during dinner, but he had made no attempt to approach her before the meal or to sit at her table. *Maybe he's forgotten about that walk*, she thought hopefully. She didn't think she could manage another half-hour tramp today, even though an evening walk was highly recommended, if not compulsory.

She nibbled listlessly at her poached chicken breast and steamed green beans, feeling so tired it was an ef-

fort to lift her fork. What with three half-hour walks,
a yoga class, the seminar with Carrie, an hour of
aquatic exercise in the afternoon and Dr. Clifford's
predinner lecture, she was pooped. During the free period after the swim she'd sat on her patio and stared at
the sea, too zonked even to read a book. She had hoped
food would make her feel better, but the dinner, though
it was tasty and beautifully presented, didn't revive her
spirits or renew her energy. *How in the world am I going
to keep up this kind of pace for four weeks?* she wondered. *After all, this is my vacation. It's not supposed
to be* all *work*.

The dining room was quiet for the duration of the
meal. Everyone looked fatigued after the first full day
of immersion in the program, and they had little to say
to their fellow participants. When the meal ended,
Verna said good-night to her tablemates and announced that she was going back to her room for an
early evening.

She started down the path, thinking how nice it
would be to get into a comfy nightgown and "veg out"
in front of the tube for an hour or so. If she could keep
her eyes open that long. Every muscle in her body
ached, and she had to concentrate very hard to keep her
sore thighs and calves moving.

The hand on her arm almost sent her soaring to the
top of the pine trees that lined the path. She gasped and
wrenched her arm away from the grasping fingers.

"Whoa, there, it's only me. Mel. I didn't mean to
startle you."

"You scared the heck out of me," she said sharply,
rubbing her arm.

"I'm sorry."

"That's okay. I guess I've been living in a big city for too long. I didn't hear you behind me. I was woolgathering."

"About what?"

"How nice it will be to go back to my room and collapse."

"Aren't we going for a walk?"

"Walk?" she asked numbly.

"You know, when you put one foot in front of the other and go forward."

"That rings a bell somewhere," she said with a weary smile.

"How about just a short one? I'm a little tired myself after today," he admitted.

The meal she'd just eaten must have started to pep her up. She felt a new spurt of energy coming on. "Okay. But just a short one," Verna cautioned. She had no idea how long this second wind would last. Also, it would be dark soon. The sun had already set and dusk was deepening quickly.

"How about the beach?"

"My calves are too sore. I couldn't take having my feet sink into the sand anymore."

"I've got an idea. Let's drive into Harbour Town and take a stroll there."

"Well," Verna hedged, "I hear there are restaurants and food shops there. Maybe it would be better to stay away from temptation."

"We don't have to go near them. We can go down to the marina and look at the boats."

"All right," she agreed. "We can keep each other honest as far as the restaurants and food shops are concerned. No sneaking in for a quick pizza or an ice-cream cone."

"Or a double bacon cheeseburger and a large order of fries. And some onion rings."

"Right, none of that."

"Shall we shake on it?" Mel thrust a hand at her.

When Verna put her hand in his, he held on to it for a moment longer than was necessary, but only a moment—more an invitation than a demand.

"It's a deal. We look at boats only. No banana boats."

Verna looked at him quizzically. "Why would we want to look at a boat that hauls bananas? How many bananas could we eat?"

"I wasn't thinking of boats that carry bananas," he explained as they walked to the parking lot. "I was thinking of banana splits. You know, with ice cream and crushed pineapple and hot fudge and whipped cream with a cherry on top. Haven't you ever heard them called banana boats?"

"No," she replied. "I can't say that I have." His description of the ice-cream concoction had set her mind on an unhealthy track. She could see herself spooning up a big mouthful. That kind of thinking wasn't going to help her melt away her unwanted pounds. "Can we talk about something besides food?" she asked.

"Sure," he replied amiably. They reached his car, and he helped her into the passenger seat. "What would you like to talk about?"

"How about what we did today?" she suggested as he settled himself behind the wheel. She braced herself for a hair-raising ride to town, but Mel eased out of the parking lot slowly and took the road at a sensible pace.

"Okay," he said with a laugh. "Wasn't that yoga class something? Does Sallie really expect us to tie ourselves in knots like she does?"

"Unfortunately, I think she does. I suppose we'll get the hang of it, sooner or later," she added doubtfully.

"It's a good thing there're no ropes involved. We might end up hanging ourselves. Literally." He kept one hand on the wheel and wrapped the other around his throat, accompanying his movement with chokes and gasps.

Verna chuckled at his antics. "You're very funny, you know."

"If you laugh at yourself first, it takes away some of the sting when other people laugh at you. A clumsy oaf like me ought to know."

Beneath the jollity there was bitterness and pain in his voice. Verna reached out instinctively to touch his arm. "You're not the only one. I know what it's like to be the last kid chosen for dodgeball. I probably hold the world's record." When she finished speaking, she realized she was still holding on to his arm. She removed her hand quickly, as if his arm suddenly had become red-hot.

"At least you had a team to be chosen last for," he said, keeping his eyes on the road with difficulty. Her fingers seemed to have burned his arm, and he had a strong desire to seize the hand that had touched him and kiss those fingers. But he controlled himself and continued talking. "The first school I went to was a high school. I was eleven."

"What do you mean? Didn't you go to school as a child?"

"No. My mother was forty when I was born. She'd given up hope of having a child, but then I arrived on the scene. When it became apparent that I was a 'genius'—" he said the word scornfully "—she insisted on teaching me at home. Both she and my father were scientists. He was a physicist, she was a biologist. She quit teaching and doing research to stay home with me. We'd spend all day together in the study. Then my father would take over when he came home. We only stopped for meals. That's all I knew. Books and food."

"They must have loved you very much," she said quietly. At the same time she remembered her own more normal childhood gratefully.

"Too much, I think sometimes."

"You can't love someone too much. You may do things that aren't so good for them because the love blinds you, but—"

"My parents sure had a blind spot where I was concerned. And for what? They wouldn't be too pleased if they knew what I was doing now. They both died in a car crash about ten years ago," he explained.

"I'm sorry."

"Thank you."

"But why wouldn't they be proud of you? You've done some wonderful work. Why, everyone in the country who uses a computer has heard of Peony. You've made thousands of people more productive and effective at their jobs. What's wrong with that?"

"It's not theoretical math or physics. That's what's wrong with it. They'd be shocked that I left the lab to work in the real world, to start a business. They had little trust in or respect for the world of commerce."

"There are unethical people in every sphere of life," Verna protested. "Scientists as well as businessmen. Not to mention politicians," she added, unable to leave out her own often maligned sector.

"I know that, but they tended to see things in absolutes. Let's change the subject. I didn't mean to go on about my less-than-ecstatic childhood." They had reached the town, and he began to look for a spot to park.

"It's never too late to have a happy childhood," she said lightly after a moment's silence.

Mel swerved into a parking space with a squeal of tires, spitting out words like sparks from a volcano. "I'm smart, but I'm not that smart, Verna. I haven't figured out how to build a time machine yet. And the statistical probability of anyone designing one in our lifetime is nil. I don't mean practically nil. I mean nil. Absolutely zero."

Verna sat stock-still during the first rapid-fire delivery of the evening. She must have set off the explosion with what she'd said, but she didn't understand how. "Hold on. Don't get so excited. It's only something I read in a book." She opened the car door for herself and stepped out, gratefully inhaling the cool evening air. The atmosphere in the car had become uncomfortably warm.

"What book?" he asked suspiciously, hurrying around from his side of the car.

"Something by Tom Robbins," she answered. "*Still Life with Woodpecker*, I think."

"What kind of title is that?"

"Whimsical. Like the advice, Mel. It doesn't mean you literally have to go back to your childhood but that you can rewrite it in the present, if you want to."

"Pretend it didn't happen?" he scoffed. "Wipe the slate clean?"

"Not at all. Just invent another childhood for yourself, make it come out the way you want this time."

They crossed the street and headed in the direction of Harbour Town's famous red-and-white-striped lighthouse. They were so involved in their discussion they hardly noticed their surroundings. They didn't smell the tantalizing odors coming out of the restaurants, or look longingly at the ice-cream cones other strollers were licking.

"Why don't you give it a try?" Verna coaxed.

"Naw. I'd feel stupid."

"I don't believe you've ever felt stupid in your life."

"Yes, I have," he said vehemently.

"When?"

"When I first went to high school. There I was, eleven years old. I knew more math and science than most of the kids in the school, more than a lot of the teachers, but my parents had done a sudden about-face. They had finally decided it would be a good idea for me to be exposed to other kids, but there was no way I could go into the seventh grade with other kids my age. I'd've been bored stiff.

"I'm not sure the boredom could have been much worse than what I found in high school. It was a disaster, a pure unmitigated disaster. Everyone seemed impossibly mature. The other guys in my chemistry class drove cars, they went out on dates with girls, they played on the football team or the baseball team. I had to take gym with them. I couldn't keep up. They ribbed me a lot. Not cruelly, at least not to my face. They called me The Kid. To some of them I was like a mascot, an amusing pet. No wonder I went with them to the soda shop every day after school and let them feed me fries and malteds and banana splits. It was the same old story. Books and food."

"So make up a new story," she urged.

They reached the marina, walked out onto one of the piers and settled on a bench, facing the bobbing boats and the dark sea prancing in the light of the new moon. Mel sat quietly, but she could almost hear the wheels turning in his head. As she waited, she thought about the happy childhood she would like to invent for herself. There wasn't too much she would change, she decided. Her family was close and loving; her young life had been untouched by tragedy or hardship. Maybe she'd just add something. Someone to talk to about all the books she read. Someone who understood her need to know about other people, other places, someone who shared her concern for other people and places. Someone who would make her feel not so much the one apart.

Mel's voice called her back from memories of Iowa. "I decided," he told her, "that I'd rather have a happy adolescence than a happy childhood."

"If that's what you want, go ahead."

"You won't laugh at me, will you? This whole thing makes me feel pretty foolish."

"I'll only laugh if you say something funny. How about that?"

"Sounds fair." He took a deep breath and started to talk. His voice sounded flat at first, but as he got involved in his story, it took on the faraway quality of reminiscence, even though he was making up the events right then and there.

"I'm seventeen. I'm a senior at the same high school I went to. I'm number one in my class, president of the student body, valedictorian, and I've got an athletic scholarship to college. I play baseball. I'm the best baseball player Hunter High School ever saw, the state of Maryland ever saw. Everybody thinks I've got a shot at the pros. So do I."

As he spoke, Verna felt herself being drawn into the story. Though he used simple unembroidered sentences, the scenes he created were as clear as a richly woven tapestry. She stopped merely listening to the story and became a part of it.

"Even though I'm a big shot, I'm a really nice guy. Everybody likes me. Especially the girls. I'm slim and handsome and I'm a great dancer. I ask the prettiest girl in the school to the senior prom. She is thrilled to be my date. We go to the prom and we dance until dawn. I walk her home. At her door she tells me what a great time she had. I tell her I had a great time, too. I take her in my arms. I kiss her good-night. Like this."

He circled one arm around Verna's shoulders and drew her to him. Before she knew it, his lips were pressed against hers. They were warm and sweet and soft, as affecting as his story had been. The kiss deepened, and Verna felt herself being drawn closer to him,

further into his world. "You're so beautiful," he murmured huskily and caressed her cheek.

The sweetness of the moment was so intense it was
almost painful. No one had ever touched her so gently,
so reverently. His other arm closed around her and he
pressed her close. "This is the way it should have been.
This is the way it always should be." He kissed her
again, like a man now, not a boy.

And she responded like a woman, a woman who
hadn't been held and kissed and caressed in far too long.
She wrapped her arms around his back and leaned into
his ample chest. When he finally released her, they
looked at each other uncertainly for a moment. Mel's
fantasy had created an unexpected reality, and neither
of them knew quite what to make of it.

After a prolonged, uneasy silence Mel said, "I guess
we'd better head back. It's getting late."

She nodded, unable to think of anything else to say.
They spoke little on the way back to the resort, and Mel
left her at her door with a hurried "See you tomorrow."

Too tired to dwell on the unanticipated turn the evening had taken, Verna undressed and crawled into the
bed, and she thought drowsily before falling asleep, *I
can't let that happen again. Too risky. It could lead to
things I'm not ready to handle yet. Not until I've lost at
least twenty pounds.*

WHEN MEL LEFT Verna, he rushed into his room and
slammed the door behind himself. *Of all the adolescent things to do,* he berated himself. Not kissing her.
He didn't regret that. What he regretted was not kiss-

ing her again at her door, not telling her all the crazy, insistent things that were going through his mind. How much he wanted to make love to her, how he'd fallen head over heels for her. Instead, he'd left her at her door with a "See you tomorrow." *Who writes your dialogue, Hopkins?* he asked himself acidly.

The hardest thing about his unworldliness was not knowing what to do, not knowing how to get what he wanted. His first impulse was to call Jack. Ever since they'd left the lab at Johns Hopkins to set up their own business, Mel had relied on his partner's advice for getting along in the world outside academia. But now Jack was hundreds of miles away. He couldn't call him every day to ask him what to do about Verna. At some point he had to start to figure things out for himself. This was as good a time as any. Besides, Jack had enough on his hands running the business while he was away.

Maybe there were some books he could read. Books that would tell him how to make a hit with a woman who set his blood racing. He'd go into town during his free time tomorrow afternoon and find a bookstore. Jack might be his best friend, but books were his oldest friends. He could count on them. They'd have the right advice for him. And he'd follow it to the letter.

4

VERNA SLEPT SO SOUNDLY she didn't hear the alarm in the morning. She awoke abruptly, glanced at the clock and saw that she had fifteen minutes to make it to breakfast. She dressed hastily and hotfooted it down the path. Only when she reached the dining room did she remember what had happened the night before.

Oh, dear. Mel's moonlight kiss could make it awkward for them to face each other in the daylight. She thought briefly about going back to her room, but her grumbling stomach reminded her that she was hungry and that she would need a good breakfast to help her through the strenuous morning that lay ahead.

She noticed with relief as she entered the dining room that Mel's back was to the door. She slipped into the first vacant seat she came to. He would have to turn all the way around to see her there. *This is ridiculous,* she thought as she poured skim milk over the bowl of whole-grain cereal and sliced bananas she was served. *I'm acting like a teenager. Nothing much happened. We took a stroll, we got a little carried away, we kissed. It doesn't have to happen again.* Still, she was glad to have finished her meal without attracting his attention. Quickly she set off on her post-breakfast walk.

She delayed arriving at the yoga class until the last possible moment. Unfortunately, Mel had the same idea. They nearly collided at the door.

"G'morning," Mel murmured, not meeting her eyes. Until he'd figured out how to woo Verna, he wasn't going to waste his time with attempts to woo her. That would be like showing someone a half-written program. He wasn't fool enough to do anything like that.

"Hello," she mumbled. *At least he's feeling as sheepish as I am,* she said to herself with some small satisfaction.

"Here are our stragglers," Sallie announced, coming over to greet them. "Grab your mats, you two, we're ready to start."

Verna and Mel each took a mat from the pile in the corner and proceeded to opposite corners of the room. The rest of the day went on in much the same way. Mel did not approach her and she did not approach him. They were civil to each other, but nothing more. By the time she made her way to her room that evening, Verna was sure that the incident was behind them and wouldn't be repeated. From now on she would concentrate on losing weight and fantasies of Jim Byram.

By Thursday morning Verna's body had begun to adjust to the increased physical activity and a diet that was low in fat and high in complex carbohydrates. Some of her muscles were still sore, but she noticed a feeling of lightness and energy. On her previous myriad diets she'd always felt hungry, tired and even deprived, but the resort's food and exercise routine seemed to be agreeing with her very well. Perhaps the difference lay in all the support she was getting—from

Carrie, Dr. Clifford, the exercise instructors, the other participants. Whatever it was, Verna was feeling better physically than she had since childhood.

During the free period that afternoon she convinced Florence to take the bike ride they'd talked about at the beginning of the week. Florence wobbled precariously when she first got on her bike. Laughing, she called out for training wheels, but with Verna's coaching she was soon pedaling along in a more or less straight line.

Florence was concentrating so hard on staying on her bike that conversation was sporadic and terse. Without talk to distract her Verna began to notice how well she was feeling. After about ten minutes of cycling she felt she was fairly flying along the paths. The day was perfect—the temperature in the low seventies, a cloudless blue sky, the sun warming her face and arms. She felt strong and free and hopeful. She realized in that moment how much her weight had been bothering her. The burden wasn't only on her hips and thighs, but in her mind, as well. With each unsuccessful attempt to lose her excess pounds, the psychological weight had grown heavier. *Maybe that's why I'm feeling so light*, she thought. *I'm taking a load off my mind as well as my body.*

"You know," Florence commented, interrupting her thoughts, "I'm actually looking forward to the first weigh-in tomorrow." Verna looked over to see that her friend had gotten over her initial difficulties and was pedaling along with confidence. "I feel I've made a very good start," Florence continued, "and I'm eager to *know* just how good a start it's been."

Because the program stressed understanding and a modification of eating patterns and exercise routines, clients were encouraged not to worry about actual pounds lost. But of course everyone wanted to know; everyone needed signposts during the journey. So during the Friday seminar everyone's weight was recorded.

"I know how you feel," Verna replied. "I'm eager to know myself. This time I feel I'm really on my way. I want to know just how far I've come and how much farther I have to go."

THE NEXT DAY VERNA WENT to Carrie's seminar with high hopes. Which were dashed when she got on the scale. She had gained two pounds! She was so flustered she could hardly speak. "I don't understand it," she said to Carrie, her voice barely above a whisper.

"Everybody's body is different," Carrie told her. "Someone who had a big loss this week may show no loss on the scales for two weeks. You know we're not after quick weight loss here. We're interested in burning off your fat and turning it into muscle. Muscle weighs more than fat, so your weight loss may be less than you originally expected. You also could be retaining water, Verna. The really important thing is how your body feels, and you've just told me you feel great."

But Verna could not be consoled. Especially when everyone else in the group had registered losses of one to three pounds. She sat quietly through the rest of the seminar, saying little, feeling as despondent now as she had felt buoyant only a quarter of an hour earlier.

When Carrie dismissed the group, she reminded them of the special entertainment that was to take place that evening. "Try not to get yourselves too tuckered out this afternoon. You've got to have something left over for the Crisco Disco tonight." On the first Friday night of every four-week program a dance band played in the lounge after dinner. The event had long ago acquired that affectionate nickname. Verna had been looking forward to dressing up, but now she decided to skip this dance and read or watch TV in her room. The last thing she felt she could do was pretend to be having a good time, but she didn't want to spoil anyone else's fun.

She left the seminar room with little appetite for lunch. She would have skipped the meal but had learned enough during the week to know that skipping meals only made you vulnerable to temptation. She nibbled at her sliced turkey and salad but couldn't finish her portion. It seemed too big, more than she could manage. She dragged herself through the rest of the afternoon—a walk, aerobic dancing. She tried to make herself feel better by making an appointment for a massage during the free period, but even that didn't dispel her gloomy disappointment.

If she hadn't agreed to dine with Florence and meet her husband, Tom, she might not have taken pains over her appearance, especially since she wasn't planning to stay for the dance. But she didn't want to let Florence down, especially since she was a bit nervous about seeing her husband after a week's absence. So she washed her hair and brushed it into graceful waves, made up her face, sprayed herself with perfume and slipped into a pale aqua dress, simply styled with a rounded neckline, long sleeves and an A-line skirt for maximum hip concealment.

As she fastened the belt, she noticed that the waistline seemed a little loose but decided it must be wishful thinking on her part. How could her clothes be loose? She had gained two pounds. She couldn't understand it. All that effort, absolutely no cheating, and she hadn't lost a single ounce. On the contrary, she had gained thirty-two. What was the use? she wondered despondently as she applied a finishing coat of dusty-rose lipstick. She'd never look like the ideal woman she had created in her head, the one with the svelte body and the designer clothes. Jim Byram would never treat her like anything more than "good old Verna." She dragged herself reluctantly to her door, anxious for the moment when she could slip back into the safe haven of her room.

MEL THOUGHT he had the techniques down pat. He'd pored over the books he'd bought and practiced what they preached all week. He'd made a list of compliments and memorized them; mugged in the mirror looking strong and protective and sure of himself; armed himself with a fusillade of topics of conversation. He'd thrown out the stupid book that had said in fifty different ways "Be yourself." He'd never get Verna that way.

He smoothed down his unruly curls once more, adjusted his red silk tie and the cuffs of his white shirt with the thin red stripe. Jack had taken him to a fancy tailor to have some business suits made, so his navy-blue suit still fitted well, even though he'd had to take in an extra notch on the belt because of the absence of three of the pounds he'd had when the suit was made. His face had a light tan from being in the sun so much. He was looking better than he ever had.

He laughed, remembering the day he and Jack had gone to pick up the suit. "You clean up pretty good, Hopkins," his partner had told him when he modeled his new acquisition. Taking a final look in the mirror, Mel had to admit that Krynicki was right. He looked pretty damned good. But not half as good as he was going to look in ten or twelve weeks, when he would be about forty pounds lighter and trim as a yacht.

Feeling jaunty, confident and ready to swing into action, Mel stepped into the lounge. To start the festive affair French sparkling cider was being served in champagne glasses. Around the room program participants introduced their visitors to colleagues and instructors. He spotted Verna immediately through the small crowd. She was wearing a dress the color of a tropical sea, and her dark blond hair rolled down to her shoulders in gentle waves. She looked beautiful to him, but even at a distance he could see that her manner was unusually subdued.

He got a glass of cider and made his way to where she stood chatting with Florence and an athletic-looking man in a gray pin-striped suit. "Hi, there," he said brightly to the group, carefully avoiding looking at Verna. Nothing turned women off faster, one of the books had said, than an aggressive come-on. *Be cool*, the author advised, *make her want to come to you.*

A glowing Florence Hathaway introduced him to her husband, Tom. "This is the man I was telling you about, the one who invented Pansy."

"Peony," Mel corrected.

Florence laughed merrily. "I knew it was some flower that began with *P*." She held up her glass. "You'd think there was champagne in here, the way I'm acting."

Verna looked fondly at her new friend. Florence had been giddy with happiness since Tom arrived earlier in the afternoon. As soon as she met him, Verna could see why Florence worried about younger women taking an interest in her handsome and distinguished-looking husband, but she also saw in the way Tom looked at his wife that he would not be inclined to return that interest. It was lovely to see a couple who had celebrated their silver wedding anniversary so glad to be reunited after less than a week's separation. Seeing Florence and Tom together, however, also reminded her that at the moment she had no prospect of celebrating a first wedding anniversary with anyone, much less a twenty-fifth.

"I'm very happy to meet you," Tom Hathaway was saying as he shook Mel's hand. "I own a small textile business, and Peony has done wonders for us. I've never seen software that's so streamlined yet so powerful."

"Thank you, Mr. Hathaway," Mel responded with pleasure. He really liked that his work was of service to people. That was so much more rewarding than the theoretical work he'd done before starting his own company.

"Tom, please."

"My jewelry business isn't big enough to need a computer yet, Mel," Florence put in, "but I hope it will be soon. But even then I don't think I'd need to have it programmed to do anything as elaborate as Peony does. Tom was explaining it to me before."

"Then I'll design you a program of your very own," Mel offered. "We can call it Pansy, if you like."

"Or how about Petunia?" Tom asked.

"If it's my program, I want to call it Purslane," Florence said gaily.

"What in the world is purslane?" Mel asked.

"It's a lovely plant with small glossy leaves and bright pink or yellow flowers. It's quite hardy and grows almost anywhere with very little care. Its popular name is portulaca. You know what it is, Tom. I planted it in that spot behind the garage where nothing else will grow."

Verna followed the conversation but didn't participate in it. She just didn't feel the breeziness the others seemed to be feeling. No one seemed to notice that she wasn't having a good time, not even Mel.

She couldn't help noticing how well he looked that night. He wore his well-cut clothes with assurance; his face was relaxed, which showed up its strong, natural lines. *He's really a fine figure of a man*, she thought with momentary longing. Then she came to her senses. *Snap out of it*, she cautioned herself, *you're only feeling this way because you're discouraged. You only want his attention to distract you from feeling so rotten. You don't need that*, she lectured herself sternly. *You can take care of yourself perfectly well.*

She excused herself and went to speak to Carrie Donohue and Don Miller. When dinner was announced, they invited her to sit with them, but as she had already promised Florence that she would eat with her and Tom, she waited for them at the door to the dining room. She was momentarily dismayed to find that Tom had asked Mel to join them at their table, but then decided it didn't matter. Nothing seemed to matter much that night.

The meal started with a salad of spinach and mushrooms drizzled with spicy herb-and-lemon dressing. It was followed by broiled red snapper, accompanied by brown rice and steamed broccoli. For dessert there was a poached pear with a sauce of crushed raspberries. With every course Tom marveled at the tastiness of the food, saying that if this was dieting, count him in.

"Don't worry, darling, this is what I'll be cooking when I get home," Florence assured him. "We're learning cooking techniques and menu planning."

"That's the one thing I'm worried about," Mel said. "I've never cooked a meal in my life, much less meals like these. But if I'm going to continue to eat well when I leave here, I'm going to have to learn."

"Someone as competent as you, Mel, won't have any trouble," Florence said. "You seem as if you can do anything you set your mind to, doesn't he, Verna?"

"If you can read, you can cook," Verna responded with a polite smile. She had spoken very little during the meal, only when asked a direct question. "That's what my mother always told us, my brothers included."

Over coffee she welcomed the sounds of the band setting up in the lounge. Everyone seemed so proud and happy to have friends and family visiting that it was making her feel her disappointment and loneliness all the more. Once the music started, she could slip out quietly. No one would miss her.

When the coffee cups had been cleared away, the diners moved into the next room. Don was standing in front of the combo with a microphone in his hand. The lights in the room dimmed, and the drummer sounded a long roll. Don took on the oily tone of a second-rate saloon singer.

"Good evening, ladies and gentlemen," he oozed, "and welcome to the long awaited event of the season." He paused for effect. "The Last Resort is proud to bring you—" a longer pause was accompanied by a soft drumroll "—the Crisco Disco! Be there or be square!"

The laughter and loud applause were drowned out as the band swung into a lively rock rhythm. Don grabbed Carrie and began to dance in the area that had been cleared of rugs and furniture.

Tom grinned at Florence. "This music isn't exactly our vintage, but I'm game if you are." He offered his wife his arm and joined the stream of people heading to the dance floor.

Verna was left standing with Mel. She was about to excuse herself when he leaned down and whispered in her ear, "You look very beautiful tonight, like a vision from a tropical island."

She was startled by the comment. He had barely paid any attention to her during the evening and now he was making flowery speeches. She knew compliments from a handsome available man were supposed to make you feel great, but mere words couldn't cut through her gloom. Mel might be looking wonderful that night and he might be single, but he wasn't the man she wanted to hear compliments from. But what chance did she have of catching Jim Byram's eye if she couldn't lose any weight, if she didn't get fit enough to be able to run alongside him in Rock Creek Park?

"I'd like to sweep you away to a tropical island," Mel was saying in breathy tones, "but since I can't do that right this minute, can I sweep you onto the dance floor?"

Dancing was the last thing she felt like doing, but it beat standing around feeling glum. Since she hadn't slipped away quickly enough, she might as well get some exercise. "Sure," she answered, though without much enthusiasm.

Mel seemed undeterred by her tone. He made a gallant little bow from the waist and held out his arm to escort her to the dance floor. Once there Verna made an effort to enjoy the music and the movement, but she seemed to have acquired an immunity to the infectious joy that surrounded her. Everyone was letting loose and bouncing away to the music, but the beat didn't rouse her.

Mel, on the other hand, jumped right in and began to boogie. From what she knew about him, Verna would have bet that he'd never been to a dance in his life, but he was taking to the music like a duck to water, dancing with his whole body. He even clapped his hands and let out a whoop every once in a while. In spite of herself, she had to smile at his unself-conscious antics. She thought of what he'd said at Carrie's first seminar, that he wanted to be the best at everything he did. He certainly approached dancing that way, and what he lacked in form, he made up in enthusiasm.

When the music ended, he applauded avidly. "Great band," he commented knowingly.

"Very good," she agreed. She was about to excuse herself when the band struck up a slow number. Mel's strong arms closed around her and held her close. He began to move in time to the music, and she had no choice but to move along with him.

"You feel so good to hold," he murmured and tightened his grip on her waist. "So soft and—"

The rest of his words were drowned out by the music. So soft and flabby, Verna completed the sentence for him. She would definitely leave when this dance was over. Let Mel Hopkins practice his seduction routines on someone else. Yet she had a strong urge to let her head rest on his shoulder, to let herself melt in his arms, to be swept away.

It's just the romantic music and the dim lights, she told herself. *And the fact that I'm feeling lonely and out of sorts. If I give in, I'll only be sorry in the morning.*

The music ended, and Mel released her gently. He put his hand under her chin and raised her face to meet his eyes. "That was wonderful," he told her. He gazed at her as if searching for pearls at the bottom of a dark pool.

"Thank you for the dance," she said, tearing her eyes away. "If you'll excuse me . . ." She took a step back, turned quickly and hurried off the dance floor.

Mel felt as if he'd been hit by a tidal wave. One minute they were dancing cheek to cheek and the next she was scurrying away. What had he done? He thought everything had gone without a hitch. He hadn't been too eager. He'd complimented her, he'd been strong and protective. He'd done everything by the book and she still ran away. *Well,* he thought philosophically, *I just haven't found the right formula yet. The equation needs some more work. But I'll do it. I'll get it to balance.*

In the meantime, however, he wanted to dance. He spotted Carrie without a partner and asked her to dance. The band played a fast driving number, and Carrie threw herself into a set of energetic gyrations, which he matched.

She's more fun to dance with than Verna, he thought as he whirled and turned. *Fast dancing, that is. No one could be as luscious to hold close and sway with as Verna.* He would see to it that he had that pleasure again. Soon. As soon as possible.

5

"WHERE DID YOU RUN off to last night?" Florence asked the following morning as they stood outside the yoga classroom.

"I felt a little tired," Verna answered evasively.

"Physically tired or tired of Mel's attentions?"

"Just weary and cranky."

"I have the feeling you've been trying to avoid him."

"I know he's interested in me—"

"Interested?" Florence exclaimed. "Like the song says, he's 'got it bad—'"

"'And that ain't good,'" Verna finished.

"Why not? Is there someone back in Washington?"

"Well, sort of. But it's not that. Mel's just not my type."

"And Mr. Sort Of is?"

"I think so. Only—"

"Mr. Sort Of doesn't think you're *his* type. So you're here to lose weight and make him realize that you *are* his type."

Verna smiled sheepishly at her friend. "You're very astute this morning, Mrs. Hathaway."

"Not really," Florence demurred. "I'd have to be blind not to notice that Mel is keen on you. There had to be some reason for you to be pushing him away. I think he's terrific, Verna, refreshingly honest and charming.

Perhaps not the most sophisticated of men, but I have the feeling he's a late bloomer in that department."

"You're a heck of a salesperson, Florence." Verna changed the subject. "Your business is going to do just fine."

"I get the message. You don't want to talk about it. Lucky for you Sallie's coming up the path, so you won't have to. Not now. But remember, a good salesperson doesn't drop a pitch as easily as this."

The two women preceded their instructor into the classroom, and took mats from the pile in the corner. Verna was aware of Mel's eyes on her the moment she entered the room. She deliberately avoided looking at him and chose a spot as far from his as possible to place her mat. During the course of the week she'd felt she had begun to get the hang of the yoga postures, but this morning she made one bumble after another. She felt self-conscious, even rather ashamed of her behavior the previous evening. Running off like that had been adolescent and uncalled for. Clumsy, just the way her body felt today.

After lunch Verna was still in low spirits. There were no afternoon activities on Saturdays, so she decided to take a long walk into town and find a bookstore to browse in. She would treat herself to a couple of books. The anticipation of opening a good book, hearing the binding crack, smelling fresh ink on clean paper, always lifted her spirits. Besides, books had the added advantage of not being edible. In a bookstore she would have no temptation to break her diet.

The weather had turned cool and cloudy, so she changed into loden-green corduroy slacks, a pale-blue turtleneck jersey and her waterproof windbreaker, just in case it did start to rain. She hadn't been into town since the night she'd gone to the marina with Mel. As she walked, she couldn't help remembering that night, how cozy and innocent a time it had been. Could it have happened less than a week ago? It seemed like ages to her. She was on the edge of town when it began to rain, a chilly fall downpour that made her wish she'd worn a sweater as well as the turtleneck under her windbreaker.

She quickened her pace and found the bookstore. A clump of shoppers had taken refuge from the storm inside the door. She made her way through the crowd and began to browse. There was a table full of glossy coffee-table books, and she leafed through one about van Gogh's work at Arles. Then she moved on to the new-fiction section. As she took books down from the shelves, examined their covers, read the jacket blurbs and sampled random paragraphs, she became aware of a tantalizing smell. Coffee, she identified the aroma quickly, and bread or pastry baking. Intrigued, she followed her nose.

At the back of the shop there was a small café, five or six tables covered with red-checkered tablecloths. There was a chalkboard menu propped on a chair at the entrance. The fare was hot or cold drinks, assorted sandwiches and pastries. Many of the patrons were reading books they had just purchased. Others were chatting quietly or simply enjoying the Mozart string quartets that issued from an invisible sound system.

What a lovely idea, Verna thought. A pot of tea or a cup of that delicious-smelling coffee was just what was required to chase away the chill of walking in the rain. She decided to choose a book and treat herself to a soothing hot drink. She needed a treat, even if drinking caffeinic beverages was discouraged by the resort.

Back in the fiction section she found that two of her favorite authors had new books out. As she couldn't decide which one she wanted more, she took both the Gail Godwin and the Anne Tyler to the cash register. The clerk put her books in a plastic bag with the store's logo on it, and then Verna went to find herself a seat in the café.

As she waited for the waitress, she couldn't help but notice what the other patrons were eating. Her mouth began to water at the sight of hot apple tart, chocolate cake covered with chocolate icing and curly chocolate shavings, warm gingerbread smothered in whipped cream. She'd been so good all week, and with so little result. What harm could one small pastry do? She saw the waitress approaching and changed her mind. She wouldn't cheat. She would be strong and order only a pot of tea with lemon.

Her resolve wavered, however, when the waitress asked if she wanted anything else. She hesitated. She could almost taste the spicy gingerbread, feel it warm her tummy, soothe her frustrations. "Yes, I think—" she began.

"Verna! What a great surprise! I figured there was an excellent chance of running into someone from the resort here this afternoon, and I was hoping it would be you. Mind if I join you?"

"Please do," she said, inordinately grateful for Mel's timely arrival.

"What can I get you, sir?" the waitress asked as he sat down.

"What are you having?" he asked Verna.

"A pot of tea," she answered virtuously.

"Coffee for me," he told the waitress.

"Will that be all?"

"That's it," Mel said cheerfully. When she had gone, he added, "Of course we'd each like four pastries and half a dozen of those croissants piled with ham and Fontina cheese. That ought to hold us until dinner. Actually, I don't really feel tempted. Eating this new way makes me feel so good that I think my nice clean circuits would overload if I ate all that rich food now."

"I wish I could say the same," Verna murmured.

"Tempted, were you?"

"As a matter of fact, you arrived in the nick of time. I was just about to order a plate of gingerbread and whipped cream."

"When I pulled up on my white charger and snatched you from the jaws of peril." He picked up a knife from the table setting and laid it on his shoulder. "I now dub thee Sir Melvin the Hefty," he intoned sonorously. In his own voice he asked the imaginary dubber, "When I'm not so hefty, can I change my title, say, to Sir Melvin the Lithe?" He switched to the deep, authoritative voice again. "If you so deserve the title, it shall be yours, Sir Melvin." He dropped the resonant voice once more. "One last thing. Could you call me Sir Mel? It sounds less formal."

Verna giggled and shook her head. "You're crazy, you know that?"

"Not crazy. Whimsical. Frolicsome. It's all your fault."

"My fault?"

"Weren't you the one who told me that it wasn't too late to have a happy childhood?"

"Guilty as charged."

The waitress brought their drinks, and Verna busied herself pouring tea—real tea-leaf tea—through the silver-handled strainer that nestled in its own little silver dish when not in use. "The Last Resort seems to be agreeing with you, Mel," she said.

"It's smoothing my rough edges," he allowed, "not to mention roughing up the ones that are too smooth."

Verna chuckled. "How did you come to be in the bookstore? I thought you only read technical manuals and scientific literature. You won't find much of that here."

"I got bored with the stuff I brought with me. I thought I'd read some regular books. Got any suggestions?" He pointed to the plastic bag she had placed on the table. "What's in there?"

She brought out the two books. "Novels," she told him.

He looked them over curiously. "Would I like either of them?"

She thought for a moment. "You'd probably like the Anne Tyler better. Her characters are quirky, unusual." *Like you*, she said to herself. "Gail Godwin's more an explorer of the modern female psyche."

"I wouldn't mind knowing more about the modern female psyche."

"You're welcome to borrow either of them," she offered. "Or we can look around the shop together and you can pick out something for yourself."

"Or we can do both," he said quietly.

"Yes, we could."

They sipped their drinks in silence for a moment.

"Where'd you disappear to last night?" Mel asked her. "I missed you. So did Tom and Florence and the rest of the gang."

Verna knew they'd get around to that uncomfortable subject sooner or later. "I'm sorry. I was feeling tired and not much like partying. I had a rather disappointing day yesterday."

"Why? Because you didn't lose any weight."

"You needn't be so polite. Because I gained weight," she said sullenly.

"I'm surprised at you. You don't seem the type of person to be discouraged so easily. You wouldn't have held on to your job for this long if you'd been a quitter."

Mel was right. She'd taken her unexpected weight gain too much to heart. How many times had she searched and searched until she found a chink in the legislative stone walls she'd run into? More than she could count. "I'm not a quitter," she told him. "But I let my expectations get too high. It must be the change of food. I felt so light not only was my head in the clouds, but my feet were off the ground, too."

"Aha!" Mel exclaimed. "Now you've gotten to the heart of the matter. The trick is to keep your feet on the ground *and* your head in the clouds at the same time. That's when things really start to happen for me. At work, I mean," he added quickly, even though he was beginning to have that same sensation with her. He'd often had it when he was hot on the trail of an elusive equation—that feeling of taking off yet remaining anchored. He knew now that she hadn't run out because of anything he'd said and done but because of her own problem. He also knew that this unexpected encounter was going better than anything he could have planned—with or without the help of those books he'd bought. He'd had it in mind to see if they had any more on the same subject, but now he didn't think he needed to.

"I bet you'd like science fiction," Verna said. The thought had come to her as he'd talked about having his head in one place and his feet in another. "I don't read sci-fi myself, but I'm sure you'd get a kick out of it."

"Let's go take a look, then," Mel proposed.

They finished their hot drinks and wandered among the bookshelves until they found the science-fiction section. After skimming through nearly every book on the long rack, Mel selected half a dozen paperbacks and a couple of hard covers.

"That ought to take care of one or two long evenings," Verna said sarcastically as they walked to the cash register. It would take her weeks to plow through that many books. When reading for pleasure she liked to read slowly, to savor every word, but she suspected Mel would gobble up the eight books like a handful of peanuts.

"If that," he said quite seriously. Compared to the heavy tomes he was accustomed to, these books seemed as light as meringue.

The clerk at the register took the books frŏm Mel. "How are you today, sir?" He glanced at Verna and smiled slyly at Mel. "I guess those books you bought the other day were helpful."

"They were okay," Mel said gruffly as he handed the clerk some crisp bills.

"What other books did you buy here?" Verna asked when Mel had been given his change and package.

"Oh, nothing important, just some technical problem I was trying to work out." He ushered her out of the store quickly, wishing he hadn't given the clerk such a hard time the other day. But he'd wanted to be absolutely sure he was getting the best books that were available. "I've got it covered now," he said confidently.

The rain had let up, but it was still gray and overcast. "Maybe we should get the shuttle back to the resort," Mel said, looking up at the sky. "I enjoy walking in the rain, but I know it's not everyone's cup of tea."

"It may not rain," Verna said optimistically. "But if it does, I don't mind getting wet. I won't melt. Unfortunately," she added wryly.

"It would make our lives a lot easier, wouldn't it?" he returned with a grin. "Since you don't mind getting wet, why don't we walk on the beach? I love walking on the beach when it's chilly and rainy. I know that's perverse, but that's the way I am," he finished with a shrug.

"I guess that makes me perverse, too, because I like walking on the beach in the rain."

"Great! We can go back to the resort, dump our packages and start from there." Mel's hand clamped on her forearm, and he tugged her toward the shuttle stop.

She had to hurry to keep up with him. "Running isn't going to make the bus get there any sooner," she said gently.

Mel dropped his hold on her and smiled sheepishly. "Sorry. It's just when I'm excited about something, I want to get started as soon as possible."

"I can see that."

The van pulled up a minute or so after they arrived at the stop. They boarded to find they were the only passengers. The weather must have kept everyone else safely indoors.

"How did you come to like walking in the rain?" Verna asked as the shuttle started.

"I did some postdoctoral studies at Cambridge— England not Massachusetts. If you don't walk in the rain in England, the chances are you won't walk at all."

"From what you've said, I thought you fell into the nonwalking category."

"I would have, but, well, there was a woman there, another mathematician, and she liked to walk. It didn't matter if it was raining or not. She said walking was the only thing that could clear her mind. I came to like it, too."

"Shared pleasures," Verna commented. "I understand."

"I'm glad I have the chance to share the pleasure with you. Even if it doesn't rain."

Verna let the warmth of his words wash over her. He really was sweet, as comforting in his way as the pot of tea had been. "What happened?" she asked, curious about the woman he had mentioned.

"When?" Mel asked quizzically.

"With you and the mathematician."

"Oh, that." He realized how long it had been since he'd thought of Gillian, so long she hardly seemed real anymore. That in itself was strange, since she'd been the one serious affair in his life. So far. "Nothing happened. I went back to the States. I started moving away from purely theoretical work. We lost touch."

"These things happen."

"You sound as if you speak from experience."

"I was engaged to someone I met at college. We'd agreed not to marry until I finished law school, but during those three years we grew apart. I'd become interested in politics and wanted to go to Washington. He didn't want to leave Iowa. So we split up."

"Do you regret it?

"No. It was a hard decision to make at the time, but it was the right one. Bill and I cared for each other, but our life together wouldn't have been one of the world's great love stories."

After moving to Washington she often wondered if she'd made the right decision. Bill had never seemed to notice her farmhouse figure, but her weight was a problem in image-conscious DC. Dates, much less romances, were few and far between, and she sometimes imagined the comfortable life she and Bill might have had in Iowa. Even though she knew she never could have settled down the way he'd wanted her to, her life was too lonely not to pine for the past now and then. She'd begun to think she never would star in a great love story of her own, but when Jim Byram appeared in the wings, she'd started writing new scenarios. She hadn't thought nostalgically of Bill once since meeting Jim.

And she didn't expect to again. The future was going to be very different, she thought emphatically.

The van dropped them off in the resort's parking lot. On the way to the beach they passed Mel's apartment first. "Let's not bother to go in," he suggested. "We can stow our book bags under the table on the veranda here."

"Fine," Verna agreed, and they took off for the beach.

They walked and walked. Mel produced two green Granny Smith apples from his lumpy tweed jacket, which they munched while he grilled Verna on the political process. She enjoyed explaining the intricate journey a piece of legislation took from idea to enactment. He asked questions that weren't obvious, that made her think, that gave her ideas for when she returned to her desk.

The afternoon passed quickly, and she was genuinely surprised when Mel showed her his watch. They would have to walk very fast to get back in time for dinner.

They were both breathing hard when they reached the resort. "I enjoyed this afternoon so much. I don't want it to end. Have dinner with me, Verna," Mel said when they stopped in front of her apartment. "Just the two of us, so we can talk some more."

The afternoon had been an unexpected pleasure to Verna, too. She wouldn't mind extending it. "I'll meet you in the dining room. I'd just like to freshen up first."

"Great," he said with a beaming smile. "Dining room. Ten minutes."

VERNA'S CLOTHES WERE DAMP and salty from the seaside walk, so she decided to change for dinner. She reached for another pair of slacks, then changed her mind and chose a black gabardine skirt and a dusty-rose silk blouse. A touch of makeup, a brush through her hair and she was ready to go. As an afterthought she added a spray of perfume and took a critical look at herself in the mirror. She looked as if she was on her way to the office, so she opened another button of her blouse and fastened a rose quartz pendant around her neck. *Heavens*, she thought as she adjusted her collar, *you'd think I was going on a date.*

She found Mel waiting for her in the lounge, sipping a mineral water by the bar. He had changed, too, into an open-necked tattersall shirt and pleated tan twill trousers. His face lit up when he saw her, and she smiled in return, thinking how utterly delightful it was not to be greeted by a man who thought of her as "good old Verna."

"Do you want a 'drink'?" Mel asked when she reached his side. "Or shall we go in to dinner?"

"That walk made me hungry," she admitted.

"And since you were so virtuous this afternoon," he said with a knowing grin, "you deserve a good meal."

"Thanks to a certain newly dubbed knight," she said as he hopped down from his stool and gallantly offered his arm.

The dining room was nearly empty because many of the clients were taking meals out with their visitors. Mel led her to a small table by the window, well away from the other diners.

"You look beautiful tonight," he said softly.

"Thank you," she answered, feeling herself flush. *This is crazy,* she thought. *I'm not the blushing type.*

There was a warming cup of lentil soup to start, followed by broiled bluefish, steamed cauliflower garnished with caraway seed and a mixed green salad.

"My stomach must be shrinking," Verna commented as they waited for desert. "The portions don't seem so small anymore."

"They're small enough," Mel said, "but I don't mind. I fill up quite quickly these days. I think that's partly because I don't feel so empty inside." He reached across the table for her hand. "I'm glad I met you, Verna, even if—" He paused and looked out the window.

"Even if what?"

"Even if you're not sure you're glad you met me." She started to protest, but he kept on talking. "I'd like us to be friends, Verna. And much more."

"We are friends," she assured him, touched by his honesty but unable to commit herself further.

"I don't want to be humored."

"I'm not humoring you. I wouldn't do that. I enjoyed being with you today and I appreciate the interest you take in me. Very much."

"Appreciate," he repeated glumly. "Not exactly a ten on the Richter scale."

"This conversation is making me uncomfortable," she declared. "I don't like to assign number values to feelings."

"You're right. It's just that I'm used to making assessments in terms of numbers. It's hard for me to stop."

"You're changing so many other things here, Mel. Maybe you could add that to your list."

"Maybe I could. If it would please you."

"No, if it would please *you*."

Dessert was a baked apple filled with raisins and spices, which they both spooned up in silence. Their relationship, like an inexperienced mountain climber, had established a toehold, Verna thought, and could go anywhere now—up, down, sideways, she wasn't sure about where or what she wanted—but it couldn't remain in the same tenuous place for too long.

"Funny how some foods bring back memories," Mel said. "Baked apples are like a magic carpet to the past for me. Of course, ours at home were always buried under a mound of thick custard, but that doesn't seem to make a difference. I could be sitting in my parents' kitchen right now."

"I know what you mean. For me it's breakfast smells—oatmeal bubbling, bacon frying. I'm a kid again, coming in from the morning chores."

"I'm glad I'm not."

Verna cocked her head at him. "You lost me, Mel."

"Glad I'm not in my parents' kitchen. I'd much rather be where I am. Here, with you. I'd trade custard sauce for you any day."

"Thanks." Verna chuckled. "It's always good to know what your barter value is."

"I might even throw in some whipped cream."

"And a cherry on top?"

"Two cherries on top."

Verna finished her dessert and sat back, feeling as content as a cream-fed cat.

"Shall we have tea in the lounge?" Mel suggested. "It'll be more comfortable."

The dining room had already emptied; they were the last ones to leave. The lounge was empty, too. Verna kicked off her shoes and curled up in the corner of a couch. Mel settled himself on the other end.

"It's a lot quieter here than it was last night," he said.

"How long did the dancing go on?"

"The band cleared out at eleven, but the party went on for another hour or so. No one wanted to leave."

"Except me. I'm sorry I missed it now. Leaving was what my mother always calls cutting off my nose to spite my face."

"You don't seem to have done your face too much damage. It looks okay to me. More than okay."

"You certainly have a liberal hand with the compliments tonight."

"Only because I mean them." He thought back to the books he'd read to learn to impress her. He hadn't needed them, he realized now. All he'd needed was to follow his heart. He smiled involuntarily and started to laugh.

"What's so funny?"

His words were punctuated by laughs as he answered her question. "Remember this afternoon in the bookstore, when the clerk asked me if the books I'd bought had been useful? They were books about how to impress women."

Verna was momentarily disarmed by his confession, then she joined in his laughter. "Oh, Mel, you didn't."

"I did! I was desperate. I wanted so much for you to like me. I wanted to be cool and smooth." He stopped laughing and put a warm hand on her ankle. "I think you like me now. But I'm never going to be cool and smooth."

"I should hope not," she said fervently.

He moved closer to her and took her hands in his. "I've missed so many things in my life, Verna. I didn't want you to be one of them."

"We all miss things. We can't be everywhere or do everything, so we make choices."

"Or have choices made for us. I let other people make my choices for far too long. I don't want to do that anymore."

"Then you won't," she said simply.

He slipped his hands around her waist, drew her close and pressed his head against her soft breasts. "I wish there was music tonight. I'd love to dance with you again."

"We could pretend there's music." Verna spoke quietly.

"We could." Mel stood and held out his arms to her. The room was absolutely quiet, yet it seemed filled with a sound that was like the pounding of surf in her ears. They began to move slowly, yet in the same rhythm, to the same inaudible music. His grip was strong and comforting; he was a tower she could lean on. She rarely allowed herself the luxury of leaning, had always been adamant about standing on her own, afraid that if she accepted help, she would never succeed in her own right. But she felt instinctively that Mel's was not a strength that wanted to sap hers. It would support and enrich her own ample supply. She let herself lean against him, felt him respond to her closeness, felt his arms tighten more securely around her.

Cheek to cheek they swayed together, moving in small circles. Mel's hand roved up and down her back, sending shivers coursing along her spine. He rubbed his cheek against her hair, murmuring her name softly. Her heartbeat quickened, her mind floated away to a fog-shrouded never-never land where there was no sensation but that of holding and being held.

With almost imperceptible moves and without breaking the mood, Mel danced them over to the door. He stopped moving and pressed his lips to hers. He held the nape of her neck in one hand and ran his fingers through her hair with the other. He nibbled delicately on her lower lip, slipped his tongue through her parted teeth, tantalizing her with rapid darting passes. "Let's go someplace where we can really be alone," he whispered urgently.

"I can't," she answered dreamily.

"Why not?" he asked tensely. She couldn't take him this far and then leave. He didn't know if he could stand it.

"My shoes are over by the couch."

Mel burst out laughing in relief. "Wait right there, Cinderella. Prince Charming to the rescue."

"That's twice in one day. Better not tire yourself out."

"Don't worry," he said as he placed her black pumps at her feet. "I've barely started."

Arms around one another's waist, they slipped along the darkened path to Mel's apartment. "It's been a perfect day, Verna. Does it have to end?"

"There's no reason it has to," she said, surprised at her own reluctance to let the evening draw to a close. He opened the door and led her inside.

She glanced around the room and saw that it was a carbon copy of her own—except for the computer on the desk and a strange object on the coffee table. "What the heck is that?" She moved over to examine the object more closely. It appeared to be part of a broom handle attached to the bottom half of a plastic bucket. Five lengths of string connected the handle and bucket, and the handle was marked with a series of lines running from top to bottom at regular intervals.

"That's, um, my practice banjo," Mel answered, somewhat sheepishly. He'd rigged up the gizmo to make up for leaving his real instrument behind.

"I see." She looked at the "banjo" again and shook her head. "No, that's a lie. I don't see at all. Is this a prototype for some new banjo you're inventing?"

Mel decided he'd better explain. "I left my real banjo behind, but then I had some free time and I wanted to practice, so I put this together. Now I can practice whenever I want to, without disturbing anyone." He sat on the sofa, picked up the instrument and strummed a few silent bars.

"I get it. It's meant to be like those silent keyboards that concert pianists travel with." She looked at the bizarre object again—even stranger-looking perched on Mel's knee—and couldn't suppress a giggle. "How do you know when you make a mistake?"

"That's the best part. You can't make any mistakes. I'm the greatest banjo player in the world on this thing." He patted the broom handle affectionately.

She sat beside him. "How come you didn't bring your real banjo?"

"Well... I didn't want to disturb anyone. I make a lot of bloopers on the real McCoy."

"You mean you didn't want anyone to hear you playing less than perfectly," she chided gently.

"Yeah, I guess so. Silly, I suppose. But that's how I feel."

"Well, you shouldn't. It's not what you do that counts, Mel, it's what you are. And you are a talented, funny, kind, caring person. You don't have to be perfect at everything. Doing what you do with your own particular brand of humor and enthusiasm is more than sufficient." She realized as she spoke how much she meant every word she was saying.

He reached for her hand and gave it a hard squeeze. "Thanks. You really know how to make a guy feel swell."

"Do I?"

"Yes, you do," he said, gazing at her intently.

She looked back at him, feeling a connection grow between them, as strong and taut as the steel strings on a banjo, needing only to be strummed to make a heart-stirring sound. "It's too bad," she said quietly, "you didn't bring your real banjo. You could have played something for me."

"I can do that now. Listen carefully, and you'll see how much I've improved." He grinned at her and began to play "Oh, Susannah," imitating the thrumming sounds of a banjo. "Brum, brum, bree brum," he sang, becoming more and more animated as the song progressed.

Verna started to sing along with him. He stood, propped his foot on the coffee table, strummed harder, brummed louder. Laughing, she got up, clapped her hands and began to square dance with an imaginary partner. Soon they were both breathless and dissolved into giggles.

Mel tossed his "banjo" on the couch and hooked his arm through hers. Still humming, he swung her around one way, caught her other arm and swung her in the opposite direction. He did it once more, but this time caught her in both his arms and brought his mouth down on hers. He kissed her passionately, with a desire so strong the heat of it seemed to penetrate her lips. His fire sparked the one in her. The kindling had been laid during the day, and his kiss was the match that ignited it. She felt herself begin to smolder, to glow. She tightened her arms around him, responded ardently to his searching mouth.

"You are delicious," he murmured. "Delectable. Delightful."

Forging a trail with kisses, he moved his lips over her chin, down her neck and beside her pendant. Her skin burned from his touch, making the cool crystal that rested there feel like an ice cube, so cold it burned her, too. His mouth came to rest just above the rise of her breasts, where the silk of her blouse ended. Eagerly he kissed the soft exposed skin.

"Stay with me tonight," Mel whispered. He looked up into her face, more sure of himself than he'd ever been. He wanted her, and he would have her. His hands trailed down over her shoulders, brushing her breasts. He felt her nipples engorge and strain the silken fabric of her blouse. He wrapped his arms around her waist. "I want to make love with you. So much."

The wonder in his eyes nearly took her breath away. To mean so much, to be wanted so much, was a powerful feeling, the ultimate seduction.

"Come," he invited and took a step backward, never taking his eyes off her. She hesitated for the merest of seconds. "What's the matter?" he asked, sensing her equivocation.

"I'm not sure I'm ready for this."

He kissed her again, darted his tongue into her mouth, felt her immediate reaction. "Yes, you are," he murmured.

She was aware of how quickly and unequivocally she responded to him, but she was unsure of her body, uncomfortable about letting him see, touch, feel, all of her. "I'm afraid I won't please you. I'm still fat," she blurted out.

"I'm not exactly Mr. America myself." He tenderly stroked her hair. "Why should that keep us from pleasure? From love? I want you, Verna. Just the way you are."

And he did. He didn't care if she was thirty pounds overweight. Form didn't matter to him. Substance did. "You sure know how to make a woman feel swell," she echoed.

"You ain't seen nothin' yet." He led her into the bedroom, sat with her on the edge of the bed. He cuddled her, one arm wound tightly around her shoulders. With the other he reached for the bedside lamp.

"Please don't put that on," she whispered.

"I want to see you."

"No. Let it stay dark, then we can pretend our bodies look the way we want them to look."

"I don't want to pretend," he said fiercely. "I want to live now. No more postponements."

"You'll be disappointed."

"You might be, too. I'm willing to risk that."

What am I saying? Verna thought. *Here's a man who wants me just the way I am, not the way I might be another day.* "So am I," she said, putting her arms around him and resting her head on his shoulder.

He clicked the light on and kissed her lightly on the forehead. "You're very beautiful. Today. Tomorrow. Yesterday. To me you're beautiful."

"Oh, Mel," Verna sighed. She leaned against him, listening to the thump-thumping of his heart. The hiss of his breathing grew more shallow with every inhalation. His hand strayed to the buttons of her blouse and slowly unfastened them. He parted the silk and cupped a breast with his hand, letting out a small groan as he fondled her through the lacy fabric of her bra.

He slipped the blouse off her shoulders and sat back to look at her for a long moment. "You're lovely." He reached around to unclasp her bra. "May I?"

Her heart speeded up, but she nodded her assent. The top half of her body didn't worry her. He removed her bra and let it flutter to the floor, then reached out to touch her naked flesh. "I hope," he whispered, "that your breasts don't change much when you lose weight." He bent and kissed each one in turn, sighing contentedly. "I don't see what you were worried about. I think your body is beautiful."

"You haven't seen the rest," she said nervously.

"We can remedy that." Mel quickly helped her out of the rest of her clothes. "You're voluptuous, that's what you are," he said, eyeing her rounded hips and stomach, the ample thighs, the tantalizing thatch of light brown curls between her legs. He had to remind himself to keep breathing as he looked at her, stretched out on the bed.

"Rubenesque, it's called in some circles," she said with a laugh, relaxing under his unwavering, admiring gaze, her body starting to tingle with excitement.

"This Ruben sounds like my kind of guy." He started to undress hastily, tossing his clothes aside haphazardly.

"Rubens," she corrected gently. "An artist."

"And you're a work of art."

He stretched out beside her on the bed, and Verna took her turn to look at him. His chest, broad and covered with a mat of dark curls that matched his hair, was strong under the excess flesh. There were "love handles" around his middle, and his legs were long, if too generously padded around the thighs. Still, he was very much a man, with the badge of his manhood straining proudly in her direction.

She was glad he had wanted to leave the light on. Lying in the dark pretending would have tarnished the honesty of the moment, the way a base metal taints a precious one. She told him that, and was even more glad of the light. Without it she would have missed the priceless look in his eyes when she spoke.

He took her in his arms and kissed her fervently, a kiss that shook her from head to toe. They both forgot any reservations they may have had about their bodies and concentrated on communicating through touch and sensation.

His hands roved avidly over he body, exploring every nook and cranny. He had the power to get under her skin, to rearrange her so completely she felt that her molecules had been restructured. She responded to his caresses in kind, running her hands over his back, his buttocks, his legs, clinging to his mouth, responding to his tongue's forays with feints of her own. He slipped a hand between her legs, found the hot wetness that was waiting for him, massaged and caressed her until she felt like a pool of liquid heated to the boiling point.

"I want you, Verna," he murmured. "I need you."

"I'm here," she whispered.

He poised himself above her and looked deeply into her eyes. She could bear the penetrating gaze for only a moment. She moaned and reached for him. He entered her and sank into her depths with a groan.

For a moment he lay absolutely still. Then he began to move, slowly at first, then with a growing urgency. She met each thrust with a growing need of her own. She was drowning in sensation and yet wanted to dive deeper and deeper into that hot seething pool. She clung to him, taking him down with her. They plunged to the depths together, searching for the bottom like treasure hunters, enjoying the search, not wanting to find the treasure too soon.

For a long ecstatic moment they were suspended just inches above the bottom. Then they hit it together, setting off reverberations that sent them both shooting up through the hot blackness. Verna emerged first with a gasp that echoed in her ears; her body recoiled with a jolt so powerful she wasn't sure she would find herself in one piece when it was over. Before that happened, she felt him stiffen and clutch her shoulders, heard him call her name over and over.

They lay in one another's arms, trying to regain their breath. Gradually the world stopped spinning and Verna opened her eyes. She found Mel looking down at her, smiling happily.

"We could show the nuclear physicists a thing or two," he said.

"I'm not so sure about that. My brain seems to be on overload."

"I wasn't talking about your brain, sweetheart."

"No, I guess you weren't."

Mel snuggled her into the crook between his chest and shoulder. With his free hand he stroked her face. She lay there, legs wrapped around his, utterly spent, utterly peaceful, without a single thought for the future or the past. There was only the present for her, for him, for them.

6

LIGHT STREAMING IN through the picture window awakened Verna early the next morning. She blinked her eyes against it, wondering why she had neglected to close the draperies the night before. Then she realized where she was.

Oh dear! She let out a slow, silent sigh as memories of the night before came back to her. She glanced over at Mel, sleeping peacefully beside her, an utterly contented smile on his face. She thought of things they had said and done to each other, and she smiled, too. But there was a ruefulness, too, and confusion. She was even a bit ashamed of herself.

How had she let things go so far? What had happened to her last night? Had she taken leave entirely of her senses? On the contrary, her body reminded her, she had abandoned herself to them wholeheartedly. All too wholeheartedly.

She knew she wasn't ready to become so involved with someone—not yet. And even if she were ready, she wasn't sure Mel was the man she would choose.

How could you have done something like this? she chastised herself. *Not only to yourself, but to Mel.* He might think she'd fallen in love with him, when she hadn't done any such thing. At least she didn't think she had. And she'd have to tell him that.

Oh dear! Oh dear! she thought again and let out a small groan. Mel stirred and rolled over toward her, looking even more contented as he brushed her lightly on the buttock. How in the world was she going to face him? The thought of it set her stomach churning uncomfortably. She had never been one for impulsive gestures. Whatever had come over her last night? She couldn't even blame it on too much wine or an impossibly romantic atmosphere.

She slipped out of bed quietly and dressed quickly. She knew it was cowardly to run out on him, but she simply didn't know what she would say to him when he woke. She hardly knew what to say to herself. Maybe if she had some time to herself she could sort it out and find the courage to tell him she'd done something she wasn't sure of the night before.

She hurried to her own apartment and headed straight for the bathroom, hoping that a long hot shower would clear her head and erase the memory of his kisses, his lovemaking. But nothing could wash that away. She was marked, indelibly marked, and she knew it. She had enjoyed—no, reveled in—making love with him, she had to admit that. But in the harsh light of day she knew she had not done the right thing.

She was no femme fatale. She didn't use men for her own purposes and cast them aside. But out of her need for companionship and reassurance she had led Mel on. She had let him take friendship one irreversible step too far. She stuck her head under the hard spray, letting the water plaster her hair to her head, waiting for the drumming of the water to drown her thoughts. But of course it couldn't do that.

The next three weeks are going to be very difficult, she realized. *I can't avoid him, he can't avoid me. What am I going to do?* She shut off the water with a hard twist to each faucet, wrapped herself in a big towel and sat on the edge of the tub. *This is some pickle you've gotten yourself into*, she berated herself.

At first she thought the pounding was in her head, a headache brought on by her problem, but then she realized it was coming from outside. The front door. She slipped into her terry-cloth robe and went to answer it. A few steps into the living room and she recognized Mel's voice, calling her name.

She had to open the door before he woke up everyone in the complex. She turned the handle cautiously, intending to open the door only a few inches, but as soon as the lock released, Mel pushed against the door and came flying into the room.

"What happened to you? Where did you go? I woke up and you weren't there. I couldn't imagine what had happened to you. Is this how people from Iowa behave? Run out in the middle of the night without so much as a word? What's going on here, Verna?"

He paused for a breath, and Verna said softly, "I'm sorry."

"Sorry? What are you sorry about? Leaving like a cat burglar? Spending the night with me? What? Talk to me. Tell me. I can't stand the suspense."

"Both," she whispered.

For a split second there was stunned silence, then he launched into another monologue. "You can't mean that. I refuse to believe that you mean that. You felt what went on between us last night just as much as I did. I didn't force you to stay with me. You came quite willingly—" he stopped abruptly and gave her a sheepish look "—if you'll pardon the pun."

She smiled wanly. "I know. I don't know how I let things go so far. I like you, Mel, I really do, but—"

"But you don't know how you managed to find yourself in bed with a fat bumpkin like me. And liking it," he added savagely.

"I did enjoy being with you last night. Honestly." She stopped, unsure how to go on without hurting his feelings even more.

"But I was the wrong man at the wrong time," he said bitterly.

"I'm afraid so. There's, um, someone back in Washington." She knew it wasn't true, but she wanted desperately to make him feel better, to feel less rejected, less used. "I'm so terribly sorry. I don't know what else to say."

"I don't know, either. I thought last night, this is it, the top, the best night of my life. I let myself think you were feeling the same thing. Well, I've learned a big lesson. Don't make assumptions. They stink."

"I feel just as bad about this as you do. Worse, maybe, since it was my fault."

"Good," he said with an angry snort. "That's some small consolation." Then his face crumpled. "I'm sorry. That was a cruel thing to say."

"Not as cruel as what I did," she answered quietly.

Suddenly he rushed to her and took her into his arms. "Hey, hey," he crooned softly. "Don't worry about me. I'm tougher than I look."

She could hear the false bravado in his voice, and it took all her willpower not to throw her arms around him in return and comfort him. And herself.

Gently she extricated herself from his embrace. "You're the sweetest man I've ever met, Mel. You deserve someone better than a hard-nosed, ambitious politician like me."

"Maybe I do. But it's you I want."

"Please, don't make this harder than it has to be."

"That sounds like my exit cue. I walk out, head held high, jaw firmly set, without looking back. Well, don't bet on it. I may not have Superman's body—yet—but inside me there's a man of steel. A man who gets what he wants. You can take that as a fair warning." He turned on his heel and strode out the door.

Verna crossed the room, closed and locked the door after him. *Now what am I going to do?* she asked herself. *Pack your things and leave* was the answer that came to mind. The only answer. Mel would forget about her, and she would forget about him all the more quickly. She hurried into the bedroom, threw on a pair of jeans and a sweatshirt, pulled her wet hair into a ponytail, tossed her things into her suitcase. She could diet and exercise just as well at her apartment in Washington as she could here. Then she'd go to visit her family for Thanksgiving and on to Des Moines as planned. Nothing could be simpler.

I'd better tell someone I'm going, she thought as she reached the door with her suitcases. But who? Florence. No, she couldn't wake her at this hour, not when it was the last morning before Tom had to return to Savannah. *It'll have to be Carrie. That's what she's here*

for, to deal with our problems. She flew down the path
to Carrie's apartment. She wanted to get there before
her resolve wavered.

"Verna!" Carrie exclaimed when she opened the
door. Despite the early hour, she was dressed in a bright
green jumpsuit and had her usual sunny disposition.
"What's the matter?" she asked, quick to pick up on
Verna's agitation. "Come in."

"Thanks. I'm sorry to disturb you this early, but
something's come up and I'm going to have to leave."

"Leave?" She ushered Verna to the couch. "Whatever is wrong will keep for a few minutes. I think you
should sit down. Let me pour you a cup of tea. You look
as if you need it." Before Verna could protest, she disappeared into the kitchenette. In a moment she returned with a mug of soothing chamomile tea. "Why
don't you tell me what's going on? Has there been an
emergency in your family or with your work?"

"No, nothing like that," Verna assured her. She took
a sip of the tea, appreciating its flowery fragrance and
warmth.

"I'm glad to hear that. So what's wrong?"

"Something happened between me and one of the
other guests, something that makes it impossible for me
to stay here any longer. I wanted to tell you I was leaving so no one would think I'd drowned or had an ac-
cident."

"Do you want to tell me about the, um, incident?"

"I'd prefer not to discuss it."

"Fine," Carrie said. "I won't press you, but I do want
to point out what you'll be missing if you go. You've
made a terrific start this week. I'd like to see you follow

through with it. You know we're interested in more than helping you lose a few pounds. You have an opportunity to change your life here, Verna. Don't give that up too easily."

"I've learned a lot this week," she said faintly. "I'll be able to carry on with the program at home."

"One week isn't enough to promote lasting change. That's why the program lasts four weeks. We think that's the absolute minimum. Ideally it should be longer, but we know it's hard enough for people to get away from their busy lives for four weeks. Please reconsider, Verna. There's also the financial aspect to think about. I'm sure you've made sacrifices to pay your fee, and it's not refundable."

"I understand that, Carrie, but it would be too embarrassing for me and, er, this other person if I were to stay." She started to get up. If she stayed there much longer, Carrie surely would talk her out of leaving.

"Please stay for just one more minute. I'd like you to do something for me. Will you put your mug down, please?"

Verna felt she couldn't refuse. Carrie had been very kind to her. She put the mug on the coffee table.

"Close your eyes," Carrie instructed. "Now I want you to imagine you have two weights, one in each hand. One is the embarrassment you have about the incident with the other client; the other is the lifelong benefits you've come here to get. I want you to weigh those two things against each other for a moment and then make the decision to stay or leave."

It took only a moment for Verna to feel the difference. Her discomfort about what had happened with

Mel, acute though it was at the moment, would pass, but she might never have the opportunity to come here again. She opened her eyes and stood. "I think I'll go back to my room and unpack," she said gravely. The decision was sure to have unpleasant repercussions. Somehow she would have to find the strength to face them.

Carrie walked her to the door and patted her firmly on the back. "You made a good choice. You won't regret it."

Verna knew that in the long run she wouldn't regret it, but how was she going to get through the day? There were no classes at all on Sunday, and the day stretched ahead of her like miles of desert sand with no oasis in sight.

She returned to her apartment, put her belongings in order and sat by the window, waiting for Florence and Tom to come out for breakfast, hoping that they wouldn't skip the meal or decide to eat in town. Finally she did hear them on the veranda next door and went out to greet them.

"Can I join you for breakfast?" she asked with a cheerfulness manufactured out of the thinnest air.

"Of course," Tom said heartily. "Where have you been hiding? We haven't seen you since you disappeared on us on Friday night."

Verna had to think for a moment about what he meant. Then she remembered the Crisco Disco. It seemed to have taken place in some other lifetime. "Sorry about that," she apologized breezily. "I was too pooped to pop."

"We weren't the only ones you disappointed," Florence told her. "A certain computer genius looked like a kid whose puppy ran away."

Verna let the comment pass. "Speaking of disappearing, where did you two run off to yesterday? Or is that too personal a question?"

"We had a marvelous time," Florence gushed. "We got in seven holes of golf before it started to pour and I didn't use a cart! We walked. I was so proud of myself. Later we went out for dinner, and I wasn't even tempted to cheat. I left food on my plate because I knew the portions were too big."

"This way of eating is catching," Tom put in. "I passed up the pecan pie for dessert, and believe me, that's a first. How did you spend the day, Verna?"

"Nothing special. I walked into town after lunch and bought a couple of books," she answered vaguely enough to stem any further questions.

Mel was already in the dining room when she arrived, sitting with Carl Hadley and his wife. She studiously avoided looking at him, and he just as studiously avoided looking at her. But she was so aware of his presence that they might have been sitting in the same chair. Somehow she managed to choke down her fruit salad, toast and cottage cheese. She refused a second cup of decaffeinated coffee and excused herself.

"I think I'll go into town for the Sunday papers," she told Tom and Florence. "I can't remember when I've gone so long without reading a paper. It's some feat for a news junkie like me."

She got into her car and drove into town, feeling relief for the first time since awakening. There was no risk of running into Mel while driving her own car. Her respite was short-lived, however, for she found herself peering apprehensively up and down the street before getting out of the car to purchase her papers. *You can't hide from him forever,* she told herself as she plopped the papers on the passenger seat of the car. Sooner or later she'd have to face him. But right now all she wanted to do was postpone the inevitable for as long as possible.

FOR THE REST of the morning Verna sat in her apartment and plowed her way through the *Washington Post* and the *Atlanta Constitution*. She read everything, even the marriage announcements of people she didn't know and the classified ads. Her hands were black with ink and her brain was bursting at the seams when she dropped the last section onto the untidy pile at her feet.

Now what am I going to do? she asked herself. Lunchtime was approaching rapidly. She had to eat. Skipping meals was not encouraged. Maybe she'd run into town for some fruit and yogurt to eat in her room.

No, she told herself resolutely. *If you're going to stay, you're going to participate in the program like a normal person. You can't live on fruit and yogurt from town for the next three weeks.* She washed her hands and face, brushed her hair and put on her makeup. No matter how ragged she felt on the inside, she could look well-groomed and put together on the outside. There was always a chance that the outer layer would sink in.

She strode resolutely to the dining room, saw with relief an empty place next to Carrie and went to claim it. Mel was sitting with Don and a couple of members of his group. He looked up when she came into the room and stared boldly at her as she crossed to the table and sat down. She could feel his eyes boring into her like lasers, but she didn't look up, didn't acknowledge him in any way. He couldn't misinterpret signals if she didn't give him any.

Her stomach was too unsettled to accept much food. She picked at her salad, managed a few spoonfuls of the split pea soup. The only thing she could get down without too much difficulty was the slice of whole-grain bread. She ate all of that and felt better for it.

After the meal she started to head for the refuge of her room, but the demands of the program didn't allow that. She'd already missed the morning walk; she couldn't let the afternoon pass without getting in some vigorous exercise. If only she knew which way Mel might go for his walk, she would go in the opposite direction. But short of asking him there was no way she could know. Then she remembered the bicycles. That's what she would do. Spend the afternoon cycling. On a bike she could get far away from the resort in very little time.

She went to the bike shed and chose a sleek red ten-speed that looked as if it could be relied on to make a fast getaway. She hopped on, bent over the handlebars and pushed on the pedals. The bike glided cooperatively down the path. Soon her legs were pumping hard, the distance between her and the resort growing steadily. After about half a mile she heaved a loud sigh of relief. It felt good to be up and about, moving ahead under her own steam.

She brought her pace down to a steady aerobic level, fast enough to exercise her heart and lungs but slow enough not to wear her out too quickly. With only a week of sustained athletic activity she wasn't ready to ride as if she were competing in the Tour de France—at least not yet—but she did want to stay out as long as possible, all afternoon if she could manage it.

Another half mile of rhythmic pedaling had a calming effect on her mind. She didn't feel as frantic as she had that morning. She even began to think of other things—her Thanksgiving visit with her family, how to make the most of her month in Des Moines. That would be an important trip for her, her opportunity to remind the party leadership of who she was, of her views and of her plans for political service to the state.

Thinking about her time in the state capitol carried her along for another mile or so. She was making a mental list of the people she had to be sure to see during her stay when she suddenly heard a commotion behind her.

There was a clatter and a pounding, and then she heard a voice shouting, "Make way! Make way for Sir Melvin the Hefty!" A bicycle shot past her, wheeled around and screeched to a halt directly in front of her. She hastily applied her hand brakes to avoid a collision.

In spite of herself, she had to laugh. Mel had kitted himself out in a homemade suit of armor, complete with helmet. It appeared to be made from aluminum foil stretched over a Styrofoam form. He had even fashioned a lance out of a broom handle and bedecked his bicycle with colorful scarves and ribbons. She forced a straight face and asked sternly, "What in the world do you think you're doing?"

"I have undertaken another daring rescue," he proclaimed.

"Mel, please—"

"I would say my piece, m'lady," he interrupted. "I desire only to divert a disaster, to save us both from making fools of ourselves."

"I'm not the one dressed in Styrofoam and aluminum foil," she reminded him caustically.

He dismounted and raised the visor of his helmet. "Come on, Verna, where's your sense of humor?"

"Momentarily out of commission," she relented. She looked at him again and began to giggle. "You really are certifiable." She got off her bike and put the kickstand down.

"Look, I'm sorry about this morning."

"So am I."

"But not about last night. Nothing could ever make me sorry about that. No matter how much you ignore me. But that's not what I came here to say. We've got to live in close quarters for the next three weeks. We might as well agree to be civil to each other. It can't hurt, and it might help."

She might not want to fall in love with the man, but she had to appreciate his courage and his sense of humor, and feel ashamed at her momentary lack of those qualities. "I agree. From now on we'll be polite and civil."

"Maybe even cordial?"

"We could probably manage to be cordial."

There was an awkward silence. There seemed to be nothing else to say, no easy way to go their separate ways. Then Mel's improvised visor dropped down on his nose with a loud clunk.

"Are you all right?" she asked.

Mel removed his helmet and rubbed his nose. "Sure. It'd take more than an errant visor to harm Sir Melvin."

"How did you construct that amazing getup?" Verna asked, shaking her head. "No, *why* is the more important question."

"Because I felt lousy this morning and I didn't have anything to do and I wanted to make you laugh and make everything all right and this idea popped into my head, so I went foraging for supplies and before I knew it, I had a suit of armor. I was going to clank over to your room tonight in it, but then I saw you taking off on the bike and I thought a trusty steed couldn't do the outfit any harm. And here I am."

He tossed out the words with the speed and force of the arm of a pitching machine. "Would you care to repeat that?" she inquired mildly.

"I'm not sure I could," he said, drawing a deep breath.

There didn't seem to be anything more to say, but they stood quietly together for another moment.

"Well," Mel said finally, "I guess I'll be getting back to the castle. Maybe take a swim in the moat. It's pretty hot riding around in this getup. Care to join me? I promise to slay all the fire-breathing dragons."

"I think I'll slay my own dragons," she said with a mirthless smile. She kicked up her kickstand with too much force. It clattered noisily against the frame of the bike. "I'm going to ride on a bit farther. Thanks for coming all the way out here. And for making me laugh. I really appreciate it." She got on her bike and pushed off. "See you later." She waved as she passed him and continued down the path.

"I'd give that mission a five out of ten, old steed." Mel addressed the bike wryly. "Well, at least she didn't run screaming in the other direction." Deflated and discouraged, he began to pedal back to the resort.

And I was the one who was going to befriend him, Verna thought acidly. Worldly, sophisticated Verna was going to play her version of Anna to the King of Siam. She remembered a line from one of Anna's songs, something to the effect that teachers learn more from their students than they teach them. She did appear to be the one who was learning most of the lessons, about humility and decency and forgiveness.

She pedaled a bit farther and came to a stop in the middle of a pine grove. She settled herself under a tree on a carpet of fragrant pine needles. Why was she being so hard on herself? she wondered. She hadn't caused the world to come to an end. She'd made a mistake, a perfectly human thing to do. Unfortunately, she'd hurt someone besides herself in making it. But beating herself up wasn't going to turn back the clock, wasn't going to change anything. The best thing to do was to learn from her error and get on with her life.

Back in her apartment she treated herself to a long bubble bath, accompanied by Gail Godwin's new novel and a tape of the Modern Jazz Quartet on her portable cassette player. She would leave the Anne Tyler book for another day. She'd had her fill of quirky characters for a while.

VERNA WAS DRESSING for dinner when there was a knock on the door. She opened it cautiously, not knowing what to expect after Mel's shenanigans on the bicycle that afternoon.

"Who were you expecting? The Boston Strangler?" Florence asked.

"You never know," she replied cryptically.

Florence sat on the couch. "I'm lonely," she declared. "Tom left about half an hour ago. I want a chocolate bar," she said plaintively.

"No, you don't. You want your husband." Verna sat beside her friend.

"And I can't have him. That's why I want a chocolate bar. With almonds."

"If only chocolate *could* solve life's problems," Verna said with a sigh. "There'd be a lot fewer unhappy fat people around. Unhappy skinny people, too."

"You're in a strange mood today, Verna. You seemed odd at breakfast, too. What's going on?"

"Nothing."

"Tell that to the marines, honey," Florence said sweetly. "Would it help to talk? My daughter says I'm a good listener."

Verna's first instinct was to refuse, to excuse herself to finish her hair and makeup, but she realized that she did need to talk to someone. "I spent some time with Mel Hopkins yesterday and, well, things went a little farther than I meant them to."

"How much farther, honey?"

"All the way farther," she answered glumly.

"There's nothing wrong with a little vacation fling, Verna. Why do you feel so guilty? It's not as if you're engaged to this man in Washington."

"Engaged? Hardly." She couldn't bring herself to mention that Jim Byram barely knew she was alive, except when he wanted an explanation of some fine point of agricultural policy.

"Then what's the problem?"

"I guess I'm not one for flings."

"I don't know about that. A fling might be just what the doctor ordered. I had one this weekend, and it was marvelous."

"But Tom's your husband," she protested.

"A minor detail, honey. It felt like a fling, and that's what counts."

She patted Florence's shoulder. "I'm not sure you're the person I should be talking to today. First you want chocolate, and now you want me to go out and have an affair. Is this the kind of advice you give your daughter?"

"Verna Myers, I am shocked. Of course not. But you're not my daughter. I can see you much more objectively than I'll ever be able to see her. Mel's crazy about you. You're here to take advantage of what's on offer. He's one of the things on offer—freely on offer, you may note. Why turn away from him?"

"Because I don't want to hurt him," she maintained staunchly.

"Or hurt yourself?"

"All right, that, too," she admitted.

"Wouldn't it be better to be honest about your limits, to yourself and to him, than to push him aside? You can't push life aside, Verna. You'll regret it. You'll always wonder about what might have been. If you find out, even if it doesn't turn out quite the way you expected, you'll know, you won't have any loose ends dragging behind you."

Verna could see the sense in what Florence was saying, but keeping her distance from Mel still seemed the most sensible course. "I'll keep that in mind, Florence," she promised. "It's almost time for dinner. Let me run a brush through my hair and we can go. There won't be any chocolate, but you can talk about Tom to your heart's content and I'll listen. How's that sound?"

"Like a very good deal. I'm not sure I said what you wanted to hear, Verna, but what I said came from the heart. I hope you know that."

"I know. This whole business might take more sorting out than I thought."

A few minutes later Verna and Florence entered the lounge. Mel was sitting at the bar sipping mineral water. The women exchanged a brief look. "I think I'd like something to drink before we go in," Florence said significantly.

Verna steeled herself, took a deep breath and followed her friend to the bar. She greeted Mel civilly and ordered a mineral water with lime. The three of them chatted stiffly for a few minutes, and then Mel excused himself. Though her heart pounded wildly during the encounter, she survived it with her pride and composure mostly intact. Maybe the next three weeks weren't going to be so bad after all, she thought as she and Florence went into the dining room.

7

FOR THE NEXT COUPLE of days Verna proceeded warily. She turned every corner with caution, in case Mel Hopkins should jump out in front of her wearing armor or a lizard skin or something equally outlandish. But he behaved impeccably, kept his distance, did not pass leading remarks or throw meaningful glances in her direction. At first she was relieved, but overnight disappointment rolled in like a dismal fog.

She woke up on Wednesday wondering why he had given up so easily. Had he suddenly decided she wasn't worth the trouble, that he didn't want her so badly after all? She told herself quite sensibly as she dressed that she couldn't have it both ways. She was the one who'd told him to go away. On the other hand he'd made her first week at the resort a lively one. He'd given her something to think about besides food and exercise and Jim Byram. Maybe Florence did have a point about a vacation fling. What *could* be the harm in it? she wondered.

Stop it, she told her reflection sharply as she brushed her hair. *Since when do you play with people's feelings? Or your own, for that matter?* Equivocation had never been a problem for Verna before. Usually she set a goal, fixed her sights on it and forged an arrow-straight path to it. But with Mel she'd been bouncing back and forth like a rubber ball. Why couldn't she make up her mind?

Mel Hopkins might not be her idea of perfection in a man, but he'd paid a damned sight more attention to her than Jim Byram. He'd noticed her despite her being overweight, despite her being a lot more likely to run for the bus than for fun. She liked being noticed, but there was a lot more to a relationship than ego gratification. There was sharing and giving. Aside from their both having ended up in the same place at the same time, what did she and Mel really have in common? Not a whole lot, she decided as she laced her sneakers.

I'd better leave well enough alone, she warned herself as she left the room. Throughout the morning, and despite her determination, the fog of disappointment hung about her head.

At lunchtime she entered the dining room alone and spotted Mel sitting by himself at one of the few empty places. She looked around quickly for another seat, saw one next to Sallie, the yoga instructor, and started for it. Somehow, though, without having consciously made the decision, she found herself approaching Mel's table. It was almost as if her feet had a mind of their own, like the unattached piano-playing hands she had once seen in a cartoon.

"Mind if I join you?" she asked.

Mel looked surprised but covered it quickly. "Not at all," he said with a tentative smile.

"How are you?" She felt impossibly awkward. What was she doing here? Why hadn't she gone to sit with Sallie? Why had her feet suddenly become more powerful than her brain? Unless they were acting on signals that had bypassed her conscious mind.

"Fine. Yourself?"

"Fine. Thank you," she added as an afterthought.

They both sipped their ice water nervously.

"The problem of being stuck here together," Mel blurted out, "is that there aren't any conversation starters. I can't even ask you what you've been doing. I know what you've been doing. I've been doing the same thing myself."

"You can always ask if I've read any good books lately. Or seen any good movies."

"Have you?"

"Actually I have. I stayed up to watch *Notorious* last night, for the fourth or fifth or ninth time. Ingrid Bergman was gorgeous," she said wistfully.

"Somehow I thought you'd be more interested in Cary Grant."

"You've seen it?" Since when had Mel become a movie buff? she wondered.

"I couldn't sleep last night, either." He emphasized the last word.

She toyed with her water glass. How had he known she'd had trouble falling asleep? Or was he making a lucky guess? Although how lucky a guess could it be? *After the paces they put us through here every day, we should be nodding over dinner, not staying up until the wee hours watching old movies on television.*

The waitress served them platters of greens and raw vegetables with chunks of tuna and a yogurt dressing. Verna seized her fork and speared a slice of carrot, feigning undivided interest in her food. Maybe the signals that brought her feet to this table had been scrambled. She shouldn't have sat with him. She should have kept her distance.

"Why did you sit with me, Verna?" Mel asked after a long crackling moment.

"I don't know," she answered truthfully. "I was on my way to sit with Sallie, but I ended up here."

"Why?" he asked again. "Pity? Guilt? Curiosity?"

She shook her head. "Ambivalence. I don't usually—"

"Neither do I," he said flatly.

They both took a few more careful bites of food.

"I like you, Mel. I really do," she said. "But I didn't come to the resort to get involved in a—" she hesitated, searching for the right word "—serious relationship."

"So how about an unserious relationship? Do you have any objections to that?"

"My, you are direct," she said stalling.

"Just because we, um, spent the night together," he started in a voice that sounded unnaturally loud to Verna.

"Shh," she said urgently and glanced meaningfully at the other diners.

"Good heavens, Verna," Mel said with a laugh, "this is the twentieth century."

"Where invasions of privacy are rampant," she said stiffly. "I'm not concerned about the raised eyebrows. I simply prefer not to have the details of my personal life broadcast on the midday news."

"You're going to make a hell of a politician someday, Verna. You change the subject with the best of them,"

Mel said mildly. "If you're finished making speeches, could we get back to the question at hand?"

Verna chewed abashedly on a piece of lettuce. He made her do all kinds of things she ordinarily didn't do. She tried hard, especially in her work, not to avoid touchy issues by changing the subject or answering a question with a question, but something about Mel made her behave like a different person. She'd read in countless books that love made people do strange things, but she wasn't in love with Mel Hopkins. Not at all. She had loved Bill, but she'd never done anything strange during their relationship. The only untoward urge she'd had where Jim Byram was concerned was wanting to throw something at him to make him notice she was alive. But that was unrequited love, which promoted its own brand of eccentricity.

"Hello, in there," Mel was saying.

She looked up, startled, not realizing how caught up in her thoughts she had been. "Sorry," she said hastily.

"I wish I knew what was going on in there."

"Nothing terribly exotic."

"I don't care if it's exotic or not. I just want to know what it is. I want to be with you, now, today. We can worry about later when it comes."

"Didn't anyone ever teach you geniuses about being aware of the consequences of your actions?"

"Didn't anyone ever teach you politicians not to weigh your every action as if it were a nugget of gold, just so much currency for exchange?"

Verna looked at him cannily. He really knew how to get at her. "Why don't we just finish our lunch and go back to being civil and occasionally cordial? I'm sorry

I came to sit with you. It was a mistake." She put down her fork and started to lay her napkin on the table.

"No, it wasn't," Mel said vehemently. "The mistake is running away now that you're here."

"You don't give up, do you?"

"You don't write computer programs unless you're willing to work out the bugs in the system. I don't think you're used to giving up, either. I bet you don't write legislation that looks like a piece of Swiss cheese."

Verna smiled. "I try not to."

"So why don't you give me a try, too? I'm a lot more fun than writing farm bills."

"You are that," she admitted.

"So does that mean you'll give us another try?" he asked eagerly.

"Only if we're both very clear that no promises are being made. Whatever happens here carries no long-term commitments. When our stay is over, we go back to our own lives. If we want to continue seeing each other, fine; if not, that's fine, too. It means that either or both of us could end up being hurt," she reminded him.

"I know what the odds are, Verna. Odds are my specialty. Beating them, too," he added with a grin.

"I wouldn't be surprised to hear you'd worked this all out on your computer—what were the odds of me talking to you, you talking to me, et cetera, et cetera, et cetera."

"No, I didn't," he said earnestly. "If there's one thing I've learned in the past week or so, it's that you can't work out everything in life with mathematical precision."

"No, and not all laws are immutable, either," she said, thinking of how the rules she'd always lived by were bending this way and that in the storm Mel Hopkins was causing in her life.

Mel shook his head in mock dismay. "Someone always comes along to 'mute' them, don't they? Maybe I'll write a science-fiction novel someday called *Invasion of the Mutated Laws*. Hundreds of law journals in libraries all over the world come to life, assume bizzare and revolting forms, wreak havoc on innocent law-abiding citizens, leaving the world in the hands of hardened crimals...."

Verna chuckled. "I know I've said this before, but you really are crazy."

"Crazy, me? Mellow Mel Hopkins? Surely you jest."

She smiled happily, feeling suddenly light and buoyant, as if she were bobbing along on the surface of life instead of belly-crawling through the sand and sludge as she had been.

"Finish your salad," Mel said, gesturing at her with his fork. "It's getting cold."

"It already is cold."

"All the more reason." He brandished his fork and attacked his neglected salad with gusto.

Verna ate, too. She'd never had a fling before, but it looked as if she was going to have one now. By choice this time, not chance. At least she thought it was choice. The only thing she wondered was how her feet had known that was what she wanted when the rest of her had been saying exactly the opposite. She heard a little buzz of warning deep in her brain but slapped it away as she might an annoying mosquito. She looked at Mel and smiled. If she was going to do this, she might as well enjoy herself to the fullest. She dug into her salad. It was delicious.

VERNA AND MEL TOOK their after-lunch walk in the woods. Mel fairly bounded along the path, frolicking like a dog who'd had only short walks for several days because of bad weather. Despite her long legs, Verna couldn't match his stride and had to ask him three or four times to slow down.

Finally she stopped short in the middle of the path. "Mel! This is supposed to be a walk, not a two-mile sprint."

He was twenty yards ahead of her and kept moving backward when he turned around to answer. "It's good for you. Keeps the heart rate up." His heart was racing with more than aerobic exercise. He couldn't believe that Verna had sat down at lunch with him and agreed to carry on their relationship. The past few days had been torture. He'd wanted to take her by the arm and talk some sense into her more times than he could count, but he had somehow managed to stick to Jack's advice: be polite, but keep your distance. It hadn't been easy going back to Jack for advice. He'd wanted to solve this problem himself. But he'd needed somene to talk to, and what Jack had proposed had worked. It was unbelievable, but the living proof was looking at him. He stopped walking backward but had to keep hopping lightly from foot to foot. He was so excited he couldn't keep still. Exuberant, that's what he was. He wasn't sure he'd ever been exuberant before. It was a wonderful feeling.

Verna ran to catch up with him. "You shouldn't be let out without a leash," she muttered dryly.

"I know," Mel answered happily. He caught her up in his arms and hugged her tightly.

She let her head rest against his chest. She'd felt somewhat calculating after they'd struck their new agreement, but now she let those feelings go, sent them floating into the sky like balloons whose strings had been cut. They had two and a half weeks left at the resort and they would enjoy them to the fullest. After that they'd go their separate ways with memories to cherish. Maybe they'd see each other once in a while—fond ex-lovers meeting for lunch or a drink. She liked the idea of having an old flame—someone she could make oblique references to, someone Jim could be just the tiniest bit jealous of. Yes, she affirmed to herself, the next couple of weeks were going to be splendid.

Mel kissed her lightly on the forehead. "We ought to be getting back. We don't want to miss aerobic dancing."

"You don't like aerobic dancing."

"Today I like everything, even falling over my own feet." He looked at her with a mischievous gleam in his eye. "Race you back?"

"No way. I don't take on the impossible; I limit myself to the merely difficult."

"I'll give you a head start," he wheedled.

"Oh, all right," Verna said with a laugh. Refusing him anything now would be like forcing a marching band to put mutes on their instruments. *Let him play all his tunes, as loudly as he wants*, she thought.

"I'll give you two minutes. How does that sound?" He started to fiddle with the buttons on his watch, the type of high-tech chronometer capable of everything except launching rockets. "When the buzzer sounds, I'll start. Ready?"

Verna wriggled her toes inside her sneakers and took a deep breath. "Ready as I'll ever be."

"Okay, I'm starting the countdown. Five, four, three, two, one. *Go!*"

Verna took off like a shot, running at full speed until the path curved and she was out of his sight. She knew she'd never beat him back to the resort, even with a two minute head start. First of all, she couldn't run that far. Yet. She had to think of something else. About a minute later an opportunity presented itself. Next to the sharp bend in the path was a thick stand of live oaks. She slipped behind the stoutest trunk and adjusted her position so that she could see Mel as he rounded the corner, but he wouldn't be able to see her. She gulped in some air and controlled her rapid breathing.

She was not wearing a watch, so she couldn't gauge how long it would take for Mel to arrive, but she listened carefully for the thump of his feet on the path. At last she heard a rhythmic clop-clopping and prepared to jump out in front of him. She listened to his footsteps and peered around the tree, waiting for him to appear.

Suddenly she felt a pair of thick paws clamp around her waist. She screeched like a banshee and jumped a foot in the air. "Thought you'd be clever, eh, my pretty?" Mel cackled, sounding like Margaret Hamilton's wicked witch in *The Wizard of Oz*. "But I've got you now, in my clutches, where you belong." He whirled her around, pressed her against the tree and covered her mouth with his.

Good thing I'd gotten my breath back, Verna thought as his lips thoroughly explored hers, *or I'd never survive this kiss.* She leaned back against the tree for support, threw her arms around him and abandoned herself to her senses. The warm musky smell of him mingled with the tang of fallen pine needles, intoxicating her. A cool breeze caressed her hot cheeks. Her ears rang with a sound like the white whoosh of the sea.

Finally Mel lifted his head. "Wanna cut class?" he asked huskily.

"Everyone will notice," she objected.

He released her, leaned his right hand against the tree, then started to kiss her cheek and the downy area in front of her left ear. "I'd almost forgotten that you've set yourself up as the guardian of personal privacy. You make me forget a lot of things."

"I'd rather keep ourselves to ourselves," she mumbled feebly. She let out a soft moan. What he was doing to her earlobe—alternate nibbling and blowing—was driving her mad.

"Precisely what I was suggesting."

"I think I need some exercise," she said weakly.

"What I have in mind is supposed to be very good exercise. The best."

She ducked under his arm and took a step away. Her ponytail had come loose and her hair tumbled haphazardly across her forehead. She pushed it back with a limp wrist. "We'll be late if we don't get going."

"You're a hard woman, Verna. In some respects," he said, reaching out to run his hand over her soft lightly heaving breasts. He took in a sharp breath and let it out slowly. "All right," he told her, "I'll take you dancing if you insist." He put his arm around her waist and waltzed her onto the path and toward the resort.

Mel brought his high spirits to the aerobics class. Usually everyone kept his or her eyes glued to Sallie during the routines, following along with determined concentration but not much enjoyment. Today Mel clapped his hands with the music, whooped when he got the steps right, applauded the others when they got the right moves, too. Soon everyone was bouncing along with the beat, clapping, adding an occasional shout to Mel's enthusiastic hooting. People weren't necessarily doing the steps any better, but they certainly were having a good time.

After the cooling-down exercises that ended the class, Sallie turned to Mel. "Do you want to teach the class on Friday?" she asked. "I could use the afternoon off."

"Can I make up my own routines?" He strung together a couple of steps and a turn, ending it with a big kick and a clap.

"Why should you do that? For this group we'll get in Fred Astaire. You should be able to teach him a thing or two."

"I should hope so," Mel deadpanned.

Florence cornered Verna on the way out of the class. "You wouldn't by any chance know what's gotten into Mel since lunchtime, would you?"

"Me?" Verna asked innocently. "Why should I?"

"I'm going to offer you some more free advice, honey. Don't take up acting." Florence gave her a squeeze and a wink and left the room.

So much for privacy, Verna thought wryly. She grabbed a towel from the pile on the table by the door and mopped her face. Aerobic dancing was a real workout when you threw yourself into it instead of worrying about tripping over your own feet.

Mel came up behind her. "Had enough dancing? You look a little tuckered out."

He was glowing with perspiration but didn't seem tired at all. "Are you plugged into some secret energy source?" she asked suspiciously. "Some little invention you whipped up in your spare time?"

"What I'm plugged into has been around for a long, long time, my sweet," he said softly. He took a towel and hung it around his neck. "And it'll be around for as long as we manage not to blow ourselves off the face of the earth with our fancy nuclear toys. In the meantime, I plan to harness as much of it as I can. I recommend you do the same." The room had emptied, and he ran a finger lightly along her jaw. "I'm going to hit the showers, then I've got some work to do and some calls to make. I'll see you at Dr. Clifford's session. Save me a seat."

He turned and was gone. She stood for a moment, stunned. Where had that burst of self-assurance come from? He seemed to have changed before her eyes. Walking out of the dining room after lunch he'd been like an untrained puppy; now he was a take-charge, in-control man of the world. What was going on here?

She headed slowly for her apartment, wondering if this fling she had embarked on so blithely would be more of an adventure than she had anticipated.

8

ON FRIDAY MORNING Verna had good reason to celebrate. She had lost four pounds in the second week. Sensible weight loss was one to two pounds a week, so she had achieved a respectable, if not remarkable, two-pound deficit from her starting weight.

"What did I tell you?" Carrie chided as she recorded Verna's weight loss on her chart. "The scale moves in mysterious ways. Good work, Verna. Next victim," she called.

"It certainly does," Verna agreed as she sat down, although she couldn't help but think that the emotional roller coaster she'd been riding all week might have had something to do with promoting weight loss.

Swept away on Saturday, confused on Sunday, relieved on Monday, disappointed on Tuesday, indecision on Wednesday morning, anticipation on Wednesday afternoon. Now, on Friday morning, she was still waiting for her fling to begin. What sort of a fling was it when the hero didn't ravish the heroine? He'd kissed and cuddled and fondled her but left her chastely at her door for two nights running. Not that they hadn't been wonderful nights—full of fun and laughter and talk about everything under the sun. But what had turned her eager Lothario into a man who was sure enough of himself and of her to leave her alone when the night was still young and promising? She glanced over at Mel, as if looking in his face for a key to the puzzle. He caught her eye, smiled invitingly, then looked away before she had a chance to break the gaze. Where had he picked up these tricks? Someone had to be coaching him from the sidelines—that was the only answer.

The class ended, and Mel and Verna strolled to the dining room together. "Congratulations," he said, walking close enough to her to brush her arm with his but making no other outward signs of affection. When they were in public, he was careful not to touch her. He took her desire for privacy seriously, for which she was grateful, but being deprived of his caresses only reminded her of how delightful they were.

"Thanks," she said. "You did very well yourself." He had dropped another two and a half pounds. He was looking better and better every day. When he reached his goal weight, Mel was going to be gorgeous. Too bad that would happen long after they'd left the resort. She'd like to see him slim and trim. But there would be the times they'd meet as old flames for that.

"Shall we go out tonight and celebrate? Dinner, maybe dancing afterward." He lowered his voice. "You can get all dressed up, pin your hair on top of your head, and later I can help you take it down."

"Who's writing your material these days?" she asked, fighting to keep her voice even.

"What do you mean?"

"I mean that two weeks ago, Mel, you could hardly talk to me without getting your tongue tied in knots, and now you're saying things like . . . like what you just said." She couldn't repeat his words; they were so hot they might burn the inside of her mouth if she did.

"It's you," he said simply. "I just say what I mean, what I feel."

The look on his face was so sincere she couldn't doubt his explanation. Still, words were one thing, behavior quite another. "And whose idea was it to leave me at my door the past two nights? After our encounter in the woods on Wednesday . . ."

He smiled sheepishly. "Leaving you alone for two days worked well enough to have you come to me that lunchtime. But after we were out of the woods, so to speak, I figured it couldn't hurt to stretch things out. We geniuses learn fast. We know how to make connections." Suddenly he turned away, shy and uncertain once more. "Besides, I wanted to make sure you didn't only want me for my body. I'm not that kind of guy."

Verna gasped and spluttered, then laughter flowed out of her in a clear stream. "Mad," she said to no one in particular. "Starkers. Absolutely starkers."

Mel looked down at his body. "Who? Me? What are you talking about? I'm fully clothed in this chic and elegant gray sweat suit. Locker-room gray I believe it's called."

"We'd better get you something to eat. Quickly. It may help to stem the brain fever."

"But not the other fever I have. There's only one known cure for that."

They reached the door to the lounge, and he opened it for her. Passing him to enter the room was like passing through a charged electrical field. She could almost hear herself crackle as she moved. She'd had no idea a mere fling would be this exciting. How would she be able to contain her feelings when she finally encountered "the real thing"?

THE REST of the afternoon passed as slowly as drops of water from a water-torture kit, but finally Dr. Clifford's lecture was over and Verna hurried back to her room to dress. Mel was to call for her at seven and they would drive to a restaurant on the opposite end of the island for an evening of dining and dancing.

Although she hadn't expected to use it, Verna had packed one formal outfit, a black crepe skirt with a sequined overblouse. The blouse was cut in a deep V to show off her ample and attractive bosom. Its length and the cut of the skirt minimized her too ample hips and thighs. With high-heeled black satin pumps and her dark blond hair twisted on top of her head, the outfit had always given her a glimpse of her ideal self—tall, commanding, sophisticated. When she had revamped her figure, she could dress with this kind of panache all the time. No more dowdy, hip-hiding suits for her. Even for work she would wear colorful, eye-catching clothes.

Verna was thrilled to note as she dressed that the waistband of her skirt was a bit loose, that the sequined blouse settled more comfortably than usual on her hips. In the mirror the changes that had begun in her body were starting to show. She was able to visualize, in a way never before possible, how she would look when she had reached her goal weight. She would never be fashion-model thin, but she would have a firm, still voluptuous body, and she would be even more radiant than she was that night. She knew some of the diance was due to anticipation of the evening ahead, but there was a new feeling inside her, too, a confidence and self-acceptance that wouldn't fade with the dawn.

"Holy cow!" Mel exclaimed when she opened the door at his knock. The new suave Mel Hopkins vanished as he stood gawking at her. "Holy cow," he repeated. "You look beautiful. Stunning. Gorgeous. Pulchritudinous."

"Thank you," she answered, beaming. "No one's ever called me pulchritudinous before. It has a nice ring to it." She'd worn the same outfit to a dinner party where she'd been seated next to Jim Byram. He hadn't told her she looked pulchritudinous. He hadn't noticed she wasn't wearing a gunnysack. But those days were drawing to a close. Soon she would be so pulchritudinous that even Jim Byram would notice. "Would you like to come in?"

As Mel came into the room, she saw that he was looking rather pulchritudinous himself, if that word could be applied to a man. He was wearing the same navy suit he'd worn the night of the Crisco Disco, only this time he wore it with a natty pink shirt and a gray, pink and blue striped tie. There weren't many men who could carry off wearing a pink shirt, but Mel had the size and manliness to do it.

"It's getting chilly out," he said. "I've warmed up the car, but you might want to bring a sweater."

She felt anything but cold, but picked up the black woolen shawl she had laid out on the sofa. He took it from her and wrapped it around her shoulders, taking the opportunity to drop a few light kisses on the back of her neck. "Shall we go?" he asked.

"I think we'd better," she said through the lump in her throat. The goose bumps on the back of her neck felt as big as goose eggs.

In the parking lot Mel helped her into the Jag, and she settled into the low leather seat. When Mel turned over the engine, she could feel its power beneath her, just waiting to be let loose. She had a similar feeling herself.

"When did you get the Jag?" she asked Mel as he eased the car into gear. In his stylish suit with his curls under control, he looked as if the car belonged to him, but she couldn't help remembering the first time he climbed out of it. In his plaid shirt and worn chinos he had looked more like the car's mechanic than its owner.

"I've wanted to have one since I lived in England, but it never seemed like the kind of car I should drive. By the time my Saab finally wore out, the company was doing very well, so I indulged my secret fantasy." He shifted smoothly and pulled out onto the road. The car reached cruising speed in seconds.

"Scratch a man deep enough and you'll find a bit of James Bond. Every time."

He reached over quickly and and clamped a hand on top of hers briefly. "Don't touch the cigarette lighter," he warned as he put his hand back on the wheel. "It's a highly sensitive infrared scanner, capable of discerning your every secret wish and desire. And the glove compartment contains a box of what looks like balloons. In fact, they are my blowup arsenal, everything I need to destroy the enemies of freedom and capitalism and get the beautiful girl. Except that I have the beautiful girl. Woman, I mean."

"So you have seen some James Bond movies," she said lightly, hoping to lead the conversation away from a more serious turn.

"I've been sheltered, Verna, but I don't live in a closet. I am acquainted with one or two aspects of popular culture."

"What's the second one?" she challenged with a grin.

"Junk food," he shot back. "Ask me anything—varieties of pizza, relative merits of various brands of potato chips, best ice cream on the East Coast. And since I met Jack at the lab at Hopkins after I got back from England, I'm not bad on gourmet foods, either. Jack's a real crazy guy—my business partner and best friend. He loves bluegrass music and blue chip food. Since I've been hanging around with him, I can tell you the best brand of raspberry vinegar, where to buy the richest *pâté en croute*, or what restaurant makes the most delectable quail in pink peppercorn sauce you've ever tasted."

"Stop," she pleaded, "you're making my mouth water. But what's a gourmand slash junk-food junkie like you going to do when you get home?"

"I'll stick to the diet," he said confidently. "I like the way I'm feeling now so much that I don't think I'll be too sorely tempted. I'm not promising sainthood outside the controlled environment, but I think I'll do all right. What about you?" He pulled off the road and began to cruise the restaurant parking lot for a space.

"I may succumb to the odd temptation. I'm only human, too, but I've learned so much here about the long-term benefits of sensible eating and exercise that I don't think I'll ever want to subject my body to binging and the sedentary life again." As he brought the car to a halt, she held out her right hand and wiggled her pinky finger at him.

"Is that some secret signal?" he asked as he turned off the ignition.

"Didn't you do this as a kid? You give me your pinky, we hook them together and then we make a pact. In this case, to stick to our diets."

"I didn't do anything as a kid except read and eat. You know that."

"I forgot."

"Meaning I'm starting to seem almost like a normal person."

"I don't want you to be a normal person or an abnormal person. I just want you to be you."

He leaned across the gap between the bucket seats and wrapped his arms around her shoulders. "I'm more myself with you than anyone I've ever met. I feel as if all the scattered bits of myself are coming together."

He pressed his cheek to hers tenderly, and she felt an enormous surge of emotion rising inside her. She put her arm around his neck and held him close for a long moment, touched to the core by his openness. She was aware, especially now in his arms, that he was very much a man, but the child in him was close to the surface, quite endearing.

He let her go, passed the back of his hand over her cheek as he sat back, gazing at her intently all the while, exploring territory in her that she had only just discovered herself. She turned away first, wanting to be more certain of her own uncharted places before she opened them up to mapmakers and settlers.

"Aren't we going to make our deal?" She waggled her pinky at him again.

"I'd link pinkies with you any day." He wrapped his little finger around hers. "Now what happens?"

"Now we say together, 'We promise to stick to our diets.' Then we tug on each other's fingers until they come apart."

They completed the ritual, and Mel looked at her contentedly. "You were right. It's never too late to have a happy childhood."

Suddenly she was struck by a thought. "You know what's really different about you? You're calm. I don't have the feeling anymore that you're sitting on a rocket prepared for lift-off."

Mel laughed softly. "Yeah, I've got my feet on the ground now. And my head in the clouds. Hey, are we going to sit here talking all night, or are we going to get some chow?"

"Chow, by all means."

Mel got out of the car and came around to her side to help her out. He linked her arm around his, and they walked through the misty night to the brightly lit restaurant. Inside the hostess led them across a plush coral carpet to a secluded table in the main dining room. From another part of the restaurant came snatches of music. The walls of the room were covered with a rich floral-print paper; the tables were dressed with cloths that matched the carpet and linen napkins in a print complementing the wall covering. The effect was sumptuous yet soothing.

A waiter in black bow tie and vest came to take their drink orders. Verna asked for a Virgin Mary, Mel for the same. When the waiter returned with their order, they toasted each other and their continued success in the program.

"As I was getting dressed tonight, I kept thinking," Mel said, "that this was a night for champagne, but I don't think I need it or want it. I feel high just sitting here with you."

Verna knew the spicy tomato juice couldn't be intoxicating her, but nevertheless, she felt light-headed, too. This, she thought, was what a fling should be. The taut anticipation in the pit of her stomach, the tingling in her limbs, the buzzing in her brain. She memorized every detail—herself, Mel, their surroundings.

They began their meal with a beautiful composed salad—carefully arranged on the plate were steamed snow peas, cauliflower florets and slices of bright red beet in a light lemon mustard dressing. Then they had grilled tuna, baked potato and steamed broccoli. The restaurant was accustomed to serving patrons of the Last Resort, so the portions were not overly large. For dessert there were poached pears redolent with clove and cinammon.

They lingered over espresso—their only transgression, but a minor one and one that would only make the night last longer. Then Mel suggested that they take a table in the lounge for some dancing. But the music was too tame for them, and the other dancers were mostly retirees who appeared to meet at the place regularly.

"I feel as if we've crashed a senior citizens' convention," Mel whispered as they plodded along to a fox trot. "Shall we try to find a disco?"

"We could," she replied noncommittally.

"Or would you like to go somewhere a bit more, um, cozy?"

"Mmm," she murmured. Even if the music and atmosphere were less than exciting, being held in his arms more than made up for it.

"Like my place?" he suggested.

"What about our after-dinner exercise?"

"That's easily taken care of, like I told you in the woods." He kissed the top of her head, inhaling the fresh fragrance of her hair. "But if you don't believe me, I can always chase you around the apartment a few times."

"I might even let you catch me."

He squeezed her very tight. "I believe you would, my sweet."

On the way home Mel let the Jaguar behave like the high-performance vehicle that it was. In no time at all they came to a halt at the resort. Mel helped her out of the car and began to walk briskly toward his apartment. Verna held him back.

"Let's take our time," she whispered. "I love walking in the night air, especially when it's misty. I can't see the world too clearly then. Normally it's all too sharp and clear for me."

"I know that. It's what makes you run—both to and away from things." He put an arm around her, and she leaned her head on his shoulders. "Just like I need to slow down and notice the world around me, you need your sharp edges smoothed."

"Are you applying for the job?"

"I wouldn't mind giving it a shot."

"You're hired. As long as you don't want to make it your life's work."

He dropped his arm and took a step away from her. "We agreed," he said sharply. "What happens between us isn't serious until we both say it is. You've been dropping hints all night, Verna. I haven't forgotten."

She took his hand and brought it to her cheek. "I didn't say you had. But you do tend to get, shall we say, overly enthusiastic at times."

Mel thought back to the how-to-impress-women books he had pored over after he'd met Verna. They hadn't been much help, but thinking about them reminded him of how green he'd been. With Gillian in England there had been no breathless courting, no urgency. They had been in comfort with one another, not in love, not even in lust. Even in bed they'd been like an old married couple, all flannel nightgowns and well-worn pajamas. "This is a learning experience for me," he reminded Verna.

"For me, too," she replied. "Throwing caution to the winds is not one of my specialties."

He took her in his arms and hugged her tight. "We could improve your rating in that area."

"We could give it a whirl."

"A whirl? Did you say a whirl?" He began to dance her around at a dizzying speed, so fast she couldn't follow him in her high heels. Her feet came off the ground, and she was suspended in his arms. The mist-covered night became a blur. She closed her eyes and let the world spin out of control.

When he put her down, she kept her eyes closed and let the world twirl around her. She clung to him unsteadily and rested her head against his chest. "I think you have just redefined the whirlwind romance."

"Good," he said as he stroked her back. "I like redefining things, changing perspectives."

"You've certainly changed mine," she said quietly.

"And you mine." He placed a finger under her chin and lifted her head slowly. He gazed long and deep into her eyes before slowly seeking her mouth. His lips were hot, demanding, insistent. The searing kiss opened a new dimension in the age-old act, and she let herself be carried out of her blurred spinning world into one where there was only kissing and being kissed, hungry, searching lips, darting, adventurous tongues. When he finally pulled away, his voice was deep with raw emotion. "Let's go in."

Arms around one another, they hurried to Mel's apartment. As he closed the door behind them with a kick, he clasped her to him and delivered another mind-blurring, soul-stirring kiss. Mouth still on hers, he unwrapped her shawl from her shoulders and left it trailing off the sofa as he backed her into the bedroom. He lowered her gently onto the bed and lay beside her. Their lips were still locked. *Maybe this kiss will never end*, she thought as she twined her arms around his neck and held him fast.

He ran his hand up her thigh, over her buttocks until he found the tie that loosened her overblouse. He slipped his hand under the blouse, let it slide slowly over her stomach, her midriff until he reached her breast. She responded to his caress with a soft groan, fought for breath as he fondled her nipple. Still he wouldn't release her mouth; he kissed her relentlessly, mercilessly.

The world began to spin again, she began to feel light-headed and limp-limbed. He moved his hand to her other breast, exciting it until her chest was heaving and she was writhing with unfulfilled passion. Suddenly he released her and raised them both to their feet. The movement made her dizzy, and she clutched at his shoulders. He steadied her and began to remove her clothes.

First he unpinned her hair. "Just as I promised," he said, running his fingers through it. He lifted her blouse over her head, unfastened her skirt and let it slide to the floor. She was wearing a slip that would have been demure had it been made of anything except black satin. "Phew," he whistled. He put his arms around her, and the fabric rustled alluringly. Mel ran his hands hungrily up and down her back, over her buttocks, up her sides. Was there a sensation in the whole universe as arousing as satin over warm flesh? He couldn't think of one as he luxuriated in the heavenly feel of her. Standing back to look at her again, he whispered, "That's fantastic," and ran his hand down the front of the garment.

"This old thing?" she asked with a blush as she bent to retrieve her skirt and blouse and place them carefully over the back of a chair. She'd never thought the slip she was wearing was particularly sexy, but obviously Mel thought otherwise. She was aware of his eyes on her, of a growing heat and need deep inside her body. She continued to undress, watching him, knowing her performance enflamed him, enflaming herself at the same time.

Mel thought he'd never seen as provocative, as intimate a scene. Certainly he'd never lived one. He enjoyed every second, especially when she kicked off her shoes and slipped out of her sheer black hose. A small gasp escaped him as she raised the slip over her head. He felt the insistent ache of arousal when she turned her back to him, shrugged out of her bra, stepped out of her panties. He raced to her and swept her into his arms.

Verna held on to him tightly. She'd never done anything like that before, calculated to excite a man. It was a new world for her. She knew how Columbus's sailors must have felt when they set out from Europe, believing that sooner or later they would fall off the edge of the earth. So would she if she didn't hang on to him.

He led her to the bed and then quickly removed his clothes, never taking his eyes off her. Her body was not the one etched in his memory. "You're different," he said. "Your body, I mean. I can see the changes since last week." Her stomach was tauter, her thighs firmer, slimmer, her waist more pronounced. She was even more beautiful than he had remembered, more beautiful than he believed she could be. He told her that.

He had changed, too, she saw. He was trimmer around the hips, his chest and arms looked stronger. "You've changed, too. For the better. James Bond, move over," she joked.

He laughed and knelt beside her on the bed. "I do enjoy being with you so much." He threw his arms around her in an exuberant gesture and crushed her to him. Need for her, held in a short and fragile abeyance, overtook him once more. He bent his head to take a breast in his mouth. With his tongue he teased her nipple to hardness; with his hand he gently parted her thighs. They fell open eagerly, willingly. Her flesh was wet and throbbing.

Verna ran her hands wildly up and down Mel's back as he excited her with probing fingers. Her entire body vibrated with sensations that were exquisite and unbearable at the same time. The center of her was hot, melting like a burning candle, yet her breasts were taut and hard. She lifted his head from her breast and sought his mouth.

Their lips met, their tongues danced a daring duet. He continued the kiss as he stretched out and straddled her. He positioned himself above her, still in full possession of her mouth. She reached down and guided him into her. Ever so slowly he filled her. She welcomed him to the deepest part of her.

When he had settled into her comfortably, he lifted his mouth from hers and took a deep, audible breath. "You feel luscious," he whispered.

She arched in response to his words, clasping him tightly. He grasped her hips and dove into her with sharp rhythmic thrusts. Each one inched her toward ecstasy, yet failed to bring her to the mark.

"Come on top of me," he murmured. Slowly, staying locked together, they changed positions. She raised herself on one hand; with the other she pushed her disheveled hair off her face. He reached up to catch a breast in each hand, caressing them tenderly as she moved up and down on him. He released her breasts and cupped her cheeks, raised his index fingers to coax her eyelids open. He gazed up at her and smiled, then wrapped his arms around her and clasped her to him. "All I want is to make you feel better than you've ever felt before," he whispered in her ear. He pressed up into her, hard and hot.

She bore down on him, feeling the full lovely length and breadth and strength of him. He stayed with her as she moved faster and faster, kept her anchored to him as she moved to a new plane of sensation where she felt herself splitting into two parts, ever wider and more divergent. Then suddenly the two parts of her came together in a crash of shattering magnitude. She cried out and clung to him, riding out the storm with only his strong arms to keep her from flying away.

A deep calm came over her but didn't last long, for he grasped her buttocks and drove high into her. She opened herself to him, met each thrust until he groaned mightily and she felt his climax. "My sweet, my sweet," he murmured between ragged breaths.

They lay in one another's arms for a long time, not moving, not speaking, hardly daring to breathe for fear they would break the spell they were under. Slowly they and the world returned to normal.

"I'd like to stay like this forever," he said softly, "but I don't think my ribs can take it."

"Are you ribbing me about my weight?" she asked in jest.

"Of course not," he replied, poking her playfully in the ribs. "I'll take as much of you as there is to take."

Giggling merrily, Verna lifted herself off him. She settled herself next to him, and he snuggled her into the crook of his arm. "I don't think I ever knew what contentment was before," he said after a while.

"And you do now?"

He caressed her cheek and kissed her lightly on the forehead. "It's what I have right this moment. Lying here with you in the afterglow of making love. I don't want anything else."

Verna stifled a yawn. "That was not a response to your pretty speech," she assured him. "It was a response to your, um, recent attentions to my physical well-being."

He stifled a yawn of his own. "Give me a couple of hours shut-eye and I might be persuaded to do it again."

"I might be persuaded to let you."

In the early hours of the morning, with dawn's light creeping stealthily through the curtains, she needed little persuasion to respond to his renewed attentions.

9

VERNA WOKE UP tightly entwined in Mel's arms, so tightly that her left arm had gone numb. She tried to move away without waking him, but she could hardly budge an inch without exerting some force, so she pressed her right hand against his chest and tried to push herself away. Her effort produced the opposite effect than the one she desired. He wrapped her up even more securely.

"Uh-uh," he murmured without opening his eyes. "You're not running out on me this morning."

"I wasn't running anywhere," she told him. "But my arm's gone to sleep. 'Roll over Beethoven,'" she said and gave him a playful push.

"Why are you calling me Beethoven?" he mumbled sleepily and nuzzled her neck.

"It's a Chuck Berry song," she told him. "'Roll over Beethoven and give Tchaikovsky some room,'" she sang, paraphrasing the words. "Recorded later by the Beatles."

"Never heard of it." He began to nibble on her left earlobe.

"Oh, you do have a lot to learn," she said breathlessly. Not only her arm but her whole body was on pins and needles now. She didn't try to push him away, however.

"Care to teach me? I'm a great student."

He ran his hand along her buttocks and cupped a warm breast in his hand. Delightful as his caresses were, he had moved so that the pressure on her left arm was even greater, She pushed away from him firmly. "It would be hard for me to teach anybody anything if I only have one useful arm."

"I see your point." He gave her another squeeze and released her.

She sat up, leaned against the headboard and massaged her arm. Running away from him, as she'd done the week before, was the farthest thing from her mind this morning. She felt utterly comfortable with him and with their open-ended arrangement. She would have to thank Florence for encouraging her not to turn away from Mel. He might not be Mr. Right, but he was definitely Mr. Right Now.

Mel settled himself against the pillows with his hands linked beneath his head. "I've just had a wonderful thought. We have the entire afternoon and evening to be together. And all day tomorrow, too. That is, if you want to," he added hastily.

"Why don't we take it one day at a time?" she suggested easily. "We shouldn't feel like we have to spend all our free time together. If we want to, terrific; if not, that's okay, too." She saw that her answer had dampened his spirits, and she slid down to snuggle against him. He perked up immediately at her touch. "Let's see what the weather's like before we decide about this afternoon. But tonight why don't we stay in and watch TV or listen to music or play cards? Something simple."

"And homey," Mel added with a contented sigh. Pulling her into his arms, he kissed her fervently but without the burning hunger and urgency for her that had gripped him during the night.

"Mmm. What was that for?" she asked when they parted.

"Just to say good morning. I'm glad you're here."

"Good morning," she replied, dropping a kiss on the tip of his nose. "I'm glad I'm here, too."

They held one another quietly for a few moments. The silence was cut by a loud gurgle from Verna's stomach. She felt herself flush. "The call of the wild," she commented.

"Must be getting close to breakfast time." He consulted his watch. "We've got about fifteen minutes."

"Fifteen minutes!" She jumped out of bed and rushed to gather her clothes.

"Whoa, there." Mel reached out and lassoed her back to the bed with his long arms. "I thought you weren't running anywhere this morning."

She held up her sequined blouse. "I can't very well go to breakfast dressed like this."

"I can let you borrow one of my sweat suits."

"I'd rather wear one of my own, thanks." She slipped away from him and started to wriggle into her fancy clothes. "Maybe I will take you up on that offer," Verna decided. She didn't feel like getting all dressed up just to undress and shower in her own apartment.

"There's a set of clean sweats in the second drawer of the dresser," he directed.

She got into his too large clothes, hiked up the sweatpants around her waist, rolled up the drooping sleeves of the shirt, then remembered her bare feet. There was no alternative—she'd have to wear her heels. She slipped into the shoes and struck a model's pose. "The latest in haute couture," she announced.

"Personally I prefer you in 'no couture,' but this get-up has its charms."

She grinned and gathered her clothes. "You have until breakfast to think of what they are." Quickly she planted a loud kiss on Mel's lips and headed for the door. "See you in ten or fifteen minutes. I'll meet you in the dining room."

"I'll count the minutes."

After she left, Mel lay still for a few moments, inhaling her lingering perfume, gazing at the still warm dent in her pillow. Scenes from the previous night raced through his mind like deer through a forest, wild and free. He had never known such complete satisfaction before. Nothing seemed to be missing.

A sudden surge of energy sent him bounding from the bed. He strode into the bathroom, turned on the shower and jumped in without waiting for the water to get warm. The shock of the icy spray only fed his electrically charged senses. An inexplicable but implacable urge sent his clenched fists to his chest. He began to beat on his chest and let out a loud, sustained Tarzan yell. He felt virile, manly, capable of anything, of everything.

VERNA WAITED DREAMILY for the water in her shower to warm, so lost in thinking about Mel that by the time she remembered to test the temperature the water had run burning hot. She yelped and pulled her hand back. She turned on the cold tap, adjusted the temperature and stood under the warm water, letting it cascade over her neck and shoulders. Its heat reminded her of the warmth of Mel's body next to hers and the heat of their lovemaking. The remembrance warmed her inside as the water warmed her skin.

She dressed in a wine-colored velour warm-up suit, with a T-shirt under the jacket in case it was warm while walking after breakfast or in the morning yoga class. Brushing her tangled hair made her think of how the tangles had gotten there—Mel's fingers running through it, their feverish couplings. She thought back to her first meeting with him, when he'd nearly run her over with his impatience. Who would have imagined he could be such a potent—and patient—lover? Would Jim Byram have that kind of stamina? Or more because he was in such excellent physical condition?

She blushed and lowered her eyes from her own reflection. How could she be thinking of another man when she'd just come from Mel's bed? She felt disloyal, guilty, until she reminded herself that she and Mel had no commitments to one another, except to be open and accepting of whatever happened between them while they were still at the resort. There was nothing wrong with looking ahead. After all, making herself more attractive to Jim Byram was one of the main reasons she'd come here. She didn't have to abandon the future because she'd made the risky leap of living in the present.

She left her hair loose, brushed on a light coating of mascara, blusher and lipstick, and put a couple of barrettes in her pocket to control her hair during the yoga session. Then she hurried off to the dining room. Mel was right about their evening's "exercise." It had used up quite a few calories. She was starving.

Through the morning's activities Verna's body felt supple and relaxed. She strode along the beach with Mel after breakfast, becoming only the slightest bit winded as she matched his longer strides. She bent and stretched in the yoga postures with more ease than she had thought it possible to achieve. Muscles that had been tight and uncooperative seemed to have loosened overnight and were willing to obey the signals her brain sent them. In the front forward bend she was able to get her nose within three or four inches of her knees. The day before it had seemed to be a foot away from the desired position. She had come a long way—emotionally as well as physically—in a very short time. Yet she felt balanced, as sure of herself as she had ever been.

That afternoon she and Mel took a long, leisurely bike ride. As they were pedaling along side by side, fingers entwined, steering their bikes with one hand, a question came to Verna's mind.

"How come you learned to ride a bike if you never did any other 'kid' things?"

"I never learned until I lived in England," he told her. "It was the best way to get around Cambridge. People there couldn't believe I had never learned how to ride a bike. It wasn't easy at that age. I felt so stupid and humiliated. There I was—I could balance equations that were pages long, but I couldn't balance my body on two wheels and some bent metal. Once I stopped worrying about my feelings, though, and put my attention on solving the problem, I learned quickly enough."

"And it's something you'll never forget. Isn't it wonderful how our bodies remember things our minds have forgotten?"

"I know my body won't ever forget how it felt to hold you and make love to you last night," he said, his voice only slightly louder than the whisper of the wind through the palmettos.

"Oh, Mel," Verna breathed. Her bicycle wobbled beneath her, and she gripped his hand more tightly.

"Will you remember?"

"Yes, I will."

He squeezed her hand and smiled contentedly at her. "Good."

That night they sat in Verna's living room, where she taught him all the card games she'd played with her brothers and sisters—War, Fish, Rummy, Old Maid. When they tired of playing those, they found an old horror film on TV, but most of it flickered by them as they made love on the sofa.

Sunday morning, after breakfast and a walk, they got back into bed, read the Sunday papers and got printer's ink all over one another. In the afternoon they swam in the indoor pool. For most of two hours they had the place to themselves, and they swam and splashed like a pair of happy porpoises. By the time they got to the dining room for dinner, Verna was so tired she could barely lift her fork.

She kissed Mel good-night at her door and firmly shooed him in the direction of his own apartment. "I need a night of uninterrupted sleep," she told him.

"I promise I won't lay a finger on you."

"Don't make promises you can't keep." Then she kissed him again and slipped in the door. Despite the early hour, she changed into her nightgown and got into bed. She read for a while but found her mind drifting. After an hour she put her book aside and turned out the light. She fell into a deep, dreamless sleep almost immediately.

During the next week Verna and Mel fell into a comfortable pattern with one another. They attended the morning's classes together, took their after-lunch exercise together. During the free time in the afternoon Mel went back to his apartment to check in with his partner and do whatever work was necessary. They met again for the lecture and dinner and spent the evening either alone or with their friends from the program. They showed up at breakfast together most mornings, and it wasn't too many days before they were regarded as an established couple.

On Saturday they took the shuttle bus into town. After lunch they went shopping for new clothes to wear to the farewell party, which Mel had dubbed the Less Crisco Disco. Verna didn't want to go into the town's most elegant boutique, but Mel insisted. He was also the one who picked out the smashing plum dress in lightweight wool with boxy shoulders, a fashionable dropped waist and tightly pleated skirt. She hesitated to try it on. It was not the sort of safe camouflage she usually wore. Her hesitation was not long or serious. She had lost more pounds and inches over the week. Mel's attentions and the care and encouragement of the resort staff had given her a physical boldness she'd never had before. Her appearance had never matched her sharpness of mind and force of personality, but they were coming closer and closer together. She took the dress and two less exciting garments into the dressing room.

To her delight and amazement her regular size was too large, She had to ask the saleswoman to bring her the dresses in the next smallest size. She saved the plum wool for last, but as soon as she slipped it over her head, felt the softness of the wool, the way the dress settled lightly on her shoulders and caressed her hips, she knew she would have to have it, even if the price did put a lump in her throat.

Verna modeled the dress for Mel. He said nothing, only gave her a single nod of approval. She asked the woman to wrap it up for her, barely containing her glee as she offered her credit card and signed the voucher. She kept seeing the tag in her mind, the number on it a full size smaller than the rest of her wardrobe. Any dress, even a shapeless burlap sack with holes for her arms and head, would have been beautiful to her if she could buy it a full size smaller. To have the size reduction, the soft wool fabric and the exquisite design all in the same garment made her want to squeal with delight. Verna tapped her foot and hummed tunelessly under her breath as the saleswoman carefully folded and boxed the dress. She didn't dare look at Mel in case she was tempted to take his arm and start dancing around the room. By exercising the utmost self-control she managed to comport herself with dignity until they left the shop.

When they were out on the street and clear of the shop's doorway, Verna kicked up her heels and gave a little shout of joy. Mel held out his arms and she jumped into them. Mel lifted her off the ground and whirled her around once or twice. Neither of them cared that passersby were giving them amused looks.

"Your turn," Verna said when he'd put her down. She tugged on his hand and hurried him down the street to an equally exclusive men's shop, where Mel outfitted himself in gray flannel slacks and navy blazer, both in sizes smaller than he was accustomed to buying.

They celebrated their purchases with a pot of tea at the bookstore café. Mel chattered away as they drank their tea, then pulled her into the bookstore aisles to scour the racks for science-fiction paperbacks he hadn't read. During the past two weeks he'd begun to devour books as he'd once devoured food.

"Once an addict, always an addict," he joked. "At least the books aren't fattening."

"Not unless you eat them."

He nibbled on the corner of one of the books they'd rooted out from the back of the racks. "Great source of fiber," he reported, "but it needs some spices and a splash of lemon juice."

She took his arm and steered him toward the cash register. "Don't be alarmed, madam—" she pretended to speak to an imaginary passerby "—he's weird but entirely harmless."

"Not entirely," he said, playing the villain. He stopped them in the middle of the aisle and kissed her soundly.

"You're right," she said as she got her breath back. "You are definitely a danger to clear and lucid thought."

On the way back to the resort he became uncharacteristically silent. His ebullience had disappeared, too.

"What are you thinking about?" she asked, wondering about the cause of his sudden mood change.

He hefted the box that contained his new clothes. "This reminds me that we're leaving here in a week."

She knocked her dress box against his. "It reminds me that we've still got a whole wonderful week to enjoy."

"And then what happens?"

She reached up and put a cautionary finger on his lips. "We'll deal with that when the time comes."

They continued in silence, and she couldn't help thinking that parting wouldn't be as easy as she'd thought when they'd started their affair. Still, there was no sense worrying about something that wouldn't happen for a week. She had opted for the present when she decided to be with Mel. She would cope with the future when it arrived.

10

THE GROUP'S FINAL SESSION with Carrie started with the tally of total weight losses. Verna's total came to ten pounds over the four weeks, a very respectable two and a half pounds a week, especially considering the inexplicable two-pound gain that had caused her so much consternation. By the time the new legislative session started in January, she would be quite close to her goal weight and would more than likely be wearing clothes yet another size smaller. She would also be more fit than she'd been since childhood, for she had learned well the physical and psychological benefits of regular exercise.

As the final totals were announced, the group became more and more raucous and excited, like the bench mates of a baseball team that is racking up the runs that will win them the league pennant. Mel was the grand-slam hitter of the group, with fourteen pounds lost. He gave Verna a rib-crushing bear hug when his total was announced.

Carrie had a hard time quieting the group but finally did manage to get them to sit and pay attention once more. "I don't want to rain on your parade," she said, "but you all need to be aware that being here has been the easy part. Tomorrow you go out there in the real world, where meals aren't prepared for you, where portions aren't controlled. There will be chocolate bars and ice-cream sundaes and bacon cheeseburgers everywhere you turn. There are going to be demands on your time and energy that will make it difficult to stick to your new eating and exercise habits. You're all going to blow it now and then. Especially with the holidays coming up.

"I try to think of it as being like falling off a horse. The important thing is to get up, dust yourself off and ride on in the right direction again. If you absolutely can't resist a slice of Aunt Kate's pumpkin pie this Thanksgiving, fine. Have a small slice, enjoy every bite and start over on Friday morning. The occasional deviation from the prescribed foods isn't going to put the pounds back on, but consistent cheating will.

"The other thing to remember is that we're always here if you need us. You can come back for a weekend refresher course whenever you feel you need it, and you can call me anytime—although please try not to make it at three in the morning." The group laughed, and Carrie held up her hand. "Don't laugh. It's happened. But you won't get much advice or sympathy from me in the middle of the night. I'll tell you to eat two rice cakes and call me in the morning."

The group guffawed and clapped. "Anyone who can eat two of those things doesn't need your advice or sympathy," Mel quipped. The bulky rounds of toasted puffed rice were filling and full of fiber and vitamins, but they were only slightly more appetizing than crunchy cardboard. Still, everyone in the group had found them useful for staving off hunger at one time or another.

For the rest of the session they discussed the problems each person anticipated having and what strate-
gies could be developed to cope with them. As they left
the classroom to go to lunch, Carrie had a personal
word of praise or encouragement for each of them.

"I'm going to miss her," Verna said to Mel as they
walked toward the dining room.

"Not as much as I'm going to miss you," he replied.

For the past two days Mel had been slipping in comments like that at every opportunity. He asked her five
times a day to talk about what was going to happen to
them when they left the resort. And five times a day
Verna put him off. She didn't want to think about it,
much less talk about it.

The truth was, she couldn't make up her mind about
him. She and Mel had become so close, had shared so
much over the past couple of weeks. She had become
more attached to him than she liked to admit, even to
herself. She wasn't sure she could just let him go when
they drove away the next day. On the other hand, she
couldn't see how he could fit into her life back in Washington. She needed someone who understood the political life, someone, to put it bluntly, who would be an
asset to her if she were to achieve her ambition of holding a legislative seat someday. Someone like Jim Byram.

"We've got to talk about it sometime, Verna," Mel
was saying. "Checkout time is in less than twenty-four
hours."

"I know that." She spoke rather more sharply than
she'd intended. "I'm sorry. I'm just confused, that's all."

"All the more reason we should talk," he persisted.

"Please, Mel. I'm not a program you can debug if you just keep working on it."

"I think you're being obstinate and selfish."

"And I think you're being overbearing and obsessively single-minded."

They walked on in silence. When they reached the dining room, Verna said, "I'd like to join Carrie and Florence and the rest for our last lunch." They had taken to eating most of their meals together at one of the small tables for two.

"Do the people of Iowa know you're an issue dodger?"

"Personal issues are entirely different from public issues."

"Issues are issues," he said flatly.

Mel and Verna said little directly to one another during the meal. The conversation was so lively, though, that Verna didn't think anyone would notice she and Mel had barely spoken to one another. Mel took off as soon as the dishes were cleared, and Verna asked Florence to take an after-lunch walk with her.

"Do I detect a few icy breezes in the atmosphere?" Florence asked as they tramped down the path to the beach.

"Mel keeps bugging me about what's going to happen between us after tomorrow."

"What *is* going to happen?"

"I don't know. I'm sure he wants to continue the relationship, but I'm not sure how I feel."

"How do you know he wants to continue?"

"He keeps dropping hints—how much he's going to miss me, how much the past couple of weeks have meant to him."

"Hmmm," Florence ruminated. "It sounds to me like he might be preparing you for a big letdown."

Verna stopped short and stared at her friend. "You mean he might want to break up with me?" She thought back to the things Mel had said to her. Florence could be right. He'd never said he loved her or wanted to marry her, had never tried to make a commitment to her or elicit one from her. "That never occurred to me."

Florence started walking again. "I'm not saying he means one thing or the other, Verna. I'm only a distant observer. Not that I haven't been curious," she admitted, "but you two have been so tight anyone'd need a crowbar to get between you."

Verna smiled ruefully. "We haven't been the most sociable pair, have we?"

"That, honey, is the understatement of the week."

"So you think he may be trying to let me down easily?"

"I'm only saying it's a possibility."

Verna fell silent and looked out at the rolling waves. It had been arrogant of her to make assumptions about Mel without giving him the chance to speak his mind. She had been so busy worrying about her own feelings that she hadn't bothered to look closely at his, even though he had offered her plenty of opportunities. She had done Mel—and herself—a great disservice.

"I haven't been very smart," she said glumly to Florence. "I felt I had a certain power over Mel because he pursued me and I was the one who gave him 'permission' to carry on the pursuit. I assumed I could withdraw the permission at any time, without allowing him the same privilege."

Florence put a consoling arm around her shoulders. "Now don't go getting all down on yourself. You aren't the first woman to make that mistake, and you won't be the last."

"I guess not," she said grudgingly.

"It's also not fatal."

"No," she agreed with a weak smile.

They walked back to the resort chatting about general things—plans for the Thanksgiving holidays, the possibility of Florence accompanying her husband on one of his business trips to Washington, Tom's imminent arrival for the dance and to take Florence home. She'd been thinking about nothing but what to do about herself and Mel for days, and the simple chat was a welcome distraction.

Back at her apartment Verna changed into tights and a leotard for the final aerobic dancing class. Then she went looking for Mel. She saw him coming down the path as soon as she opened the door. She went out onto the veranda and waved. "Hi," she called, smiling brightly at him. He looked so jaunty, in his sweats with a towel thrown casually around his neck.

"Hi, yourself."

They looked at each other for a long moment, not saying anything, smiling, taking in the other, taking pleasures in what they saw, in knowing how much they had shared.

"I'm sorry about before," Verna said quietly.

"So am I."

"I'm ready to talk anytime," she offered.

"Does that mean you're not confused anymore?"

"Not at all. It just means I've had my eyes opened in the last half hour. I wanted to come to a decision, then announce it to you, which was pretty cheeky of me, since any decisions we make affect both of us."

"That they do. Hey—" he held out his hand to her "— let's not make a big deal out of this, Verna."

She took his hand. "But it *is* a big deal."

"Only to us."

"Right," she said with a laugh. She squeezed his hand and brought it to her cheek.

"We'd better get a move on, or we'll be late for class."

She didn't know if it was what Florence had said or whether she was noticing more about him, but he seemed aloof, cooler than when she'd left him after lunch. *It must be my imagination*, she thought as they hurried along the path. During the class her mind was less on the dance routines than on Mel. She had reached that uncomfortable moment when the future became the present and the thing she'd put off had to be attended to. She watched Mel in the mirror, watched as he kicked and jumped and turned with more enthusiasm than aptitude. What he lacked in grace and polish he made up for in spirit. She began to realize just how much she would miss that spirit, the way he threw himself one hundred percent into whatever he did. For the first time since embarking on their affair she let herself think that their parting might not be inevitable.

When the class was over, she asked Mel if he wanted to take a walk with her after they'd showered and changed. He accepted with alacrity and they left the classroom. They'd taken only a few steps when Carrie came hurrying to them. "Mel, there was a call for you from—" she consulted the pink notepaper in her hand "—Jack Krynicki. He wants you to call him as soon as possible."

Mel thanked Carrie and turned to Verna. "If Jack left a message for me, it must be something important. I'll run ahead and take care of it. I'll meet you at your apartment as soon as I can." Then he rushed off.

Now that she was finally ready to face the question at hand, Mel's emergency left her feeling let down and deflated. She walked slowly back to her room and took her time showering and washing her hair. She dressed in comfortable slacks and a jersey and went to sit on her patio in the afternoon sun. She took her book along, but the tough case Martha Grimes had devised for inspector Richard Jury didn't keep Verna's mind from wandering farther and farther afield.

Eventually she put the book down and watched a sailboat scudding along hypnotically, a white triangle breaking the line where the blue of the sky met the blue of the sea. Somehow the sight of the sea and the sailboat transported her to landlocked Iowa, to Thanksgiving dinner on the farm. She and Mel were at the table together, refusing seconds and thirds as the rest of the family dug into the plentiful meal. That was the last thing she remembered thinking about as she leaned her head against the back of the chair and closed her drooping eyelids.

The shivering woke her up. She was huddled into the corner of the lounge chair, arms wrapped around herself, a poor substitute for a blanket. The sun had left the patio, and she remembered that it was almost winter, something she'd tended to forget in the island's subtropical weather. It would be plenty cold in Iowa by now, even in Washington, for that matter.

She glanced at her watch. It was after five o'clock. No wonder she felt so cramped. She could hardly move, but she had to begin getting ready soon. "Cocktails" started at six, and dinner was at six-thirty. Breathing deeply, she stretched her leaden limbs, stood and stretched some more. Suddenly she remembered that Mel had never shown up.

Inside she dialed his extension and got a busy signal. Could he have been tied up with business all afternoon? He'd been so anxious to talk to her that that could be the only explanation. Unless he'd purposely avoided her to show her he wasn't at her beck and call. But that wasn't like Mel at all. If anything, he was too straightforward and transparent.

She changed into her robe and freshened up in the bathroom. Then she turned on the television to listen to the news as she did her hair and makeup. Every five minutes or so she tried Mel, but his line continued to be busy. They'd never have a chance to talk before the dance now, she feared.

At five forty-five, just as she was ready to slip into her new plum dress, her phone rang. "I'm sorry," Mel began, "there was a major crisis with the latest update of Peony. I've been on the phone since I left you."

"I know. I've been trying to call."

"Sorry we didn't get our walk in. I'll pick you up in ten or fifteen minutes. I'm going to jump in the shower."

"Don't jump too high," she cautioned, "you might slip."

"Wise guy," Mel returned. "See you in a few minutes."

During the week Verna had returned to the boutique where she bought the dress and purchased a set of mauve undergarments, also in a smaller size, to wear beneath it. Now she slipped the soft wool dress over her head and felt it slide over the silky slip that covered her lacy bra and bikini panties. Maybe it was better that she and Mel hadn't had a chance to talk, she thought, as she adjusted the dress on her hips and fastened the belt. *Now we'll be able to enjoy the evening. Who knows, we might have said things to each other that would have turned the last evening into torture instead of a treat.*

In ten minutes Mel, his hair still damp from the shower, appeared at her door, natty in his new blazer and flannels. He gave an appreciative wolf whistle as he raked his eyes over her in her new dress. She turned gracefully to give him the full view.

"It looks even better than it did in the shop," he said.

"Maybe that's because of what I'm wearing under the dress."

He took her in his arms and pressed her to him. "And what might that be?"

"I'm not telling," she said coquettishly. "It'll give you something to think about during the farewell speeches."

He ran a hand over her buttocks and felt the smoothness of silk underneath the dress. "It certainly will." He kissed her lightly and held her close for a long moment.

During the long evening—sipping French cider, supping on a delicious seafood dinner followed by speeches and dancing—Verna had to ward off the feeling of "never again" that came to her again and again. It was more than leave-taking. She had become used to the sheltered environment at the resort, used to having Mel with her nearly every minute of the day. How would she readjust to her demanding and often lonely life? Time after time she pushed the disturbing thoughts away.

Don Miller, self-appointed disc jockey for the evening, kept the dance music going until the wee hours. When the party finally broke up, Verna and Mel went back to her room. There he made love to her slowly and tenderly, delighting in her sexy new underclothes, in the firmer, slimmer body beneath them. He kissed and caressed every inch of her, brought her to shattering ecstasy, cried out his own pleasure in her.

The afterglow of lovemaking kept them clinging silently to one another for a long time, but when eventually they parted, both knew that the time for a serious discussion could no longer be put off.

"So?" Verna said tentatively.

"So I guess we shake hands and you go back to Washington and I go back to Columbia, M D. Isn't that what you want?"

"Is that what you want?"

"I asked you first."

"I thought it was what I wanted. That's why I didn't want to talk about it. I was afraid you wanted us to keep seeing each other. I didn't want to hurt you."

"When we started seeing each other, I was pretty sure I never wanted to part, but now I think we'd be better off if we went our separate ways," Mel said softly. Only part of the crisis that had kept him on the phone all afternoon had been business. The other was what to do about Verna, which he hashed and rehashed with Jack. Until that morning he'd been willing to try to cajole her into seeing him, just as he had here at the resort. But she'd refused to talk to him one too many times. He'd spent the afternoon reconsidering. Verna might have been the first woman he fell for in a big way, but she wasn't the only woman in the world. If she didn't want him, he wasn't going to twist her arm.

"But all those things you said to me," she was saying, "about missing me and how wonderful it's been to share all that we have. Didn't you mean what you said?"

"Of course I meant them. I will miss you. What we've had has been very important to me."

"But you're willing to let it go."

"If you are."

So Florence had been right, she thought. He didn't want to continue the relationship. Well, that was fine with her. She'd had only momentary doubts that he was what she wanted. At least they weren't going to have a scene about it. "We've had a lot of fun." She was surprised to feel tears well up in her eyes as she spoke. She choked them and the lump in her throat down.

"More than fun." He took her in his arms and pressed his warm naked body to hers. "I'll never forget you, Verna." He held her for another moment, savoring the feel of her, then let her go. "Never." Quickly he pulled away from her and got out of bed.

"Where are you going?" she asked as he bent to pick up the clothes he had carelessly discarded in passion.

"I need to get an early start in the morning. I don't want to disturb you." In fact, he was thinking he'd pack up and leave right away. There was no sense in hanging around. He took one last look at her. "Take care of yourself, Verna."

"You, too, Mel."

She watched in disbelief as he left the bedroom. She listened to him cross the living room and let himself out the front door. Their affair was over. Nothing left but the memories. She had gotten what she set out to get, she thought bitterly. Then why did she feel cheated and unsatisfied?

11

AT SIX O'CLOCK in the morning Verna gave up the pretense of trying to sleep and got up to pack. She left her suitcases by the door and went to breakfast. Everyone asked her where Mel was. She told them he'd had to make an early start and changed the subject. It seemed strange to be in the dining room without him. She wondered how much stranger it would feel to be everywhere without him. She'd probably miss him for a few days, then she'd get back into the swing of things at work and he would fade to a pleasantly blurred memory. That might not happen until things started to heat up between her and Jim, but it would happen.

After breakfast she said goodbye to everyone, took a final walk on the beach and drove straight through to Washington, arriving late that night. She spent Sunday seeing to her accumulated mail, her apartment, laundry, repacking, and early on Monday morning she flew to Des Moines. She settled herself into her temporary quarters and reported to Senator Carlsen's office. The senator greeted her with her usual gruff warmth, commented on how well she was looking and proceeded to run down a list of things that had to be done—yesterday. Within an hour Verna forgot she'd ever been away. The only indication that she'd been at the Last Resort was what she ate for lunch—cottage cheese and fruit instead of a burger and fries.

She worked late on Wednesday night, accompanying the senator to a dinner meeting with a group of agricultural leaders, a duty she was glad to undertake, for it cemented her own political alliances. There was little she could eat at the meal, however. The chicken was deep-fried, the mashed potatoes swimming in gravy, the lima beans drowning in melted butter. She had found that getting the lighter fare she'd become accustomed to was not all that easy in the "real world," as Carrie had warned them, but she had learned to keep emergency rations of fruit and raw vegetables in her purse, and on the way home from the meeting she quieted her grumbling stomach with some carrot sticks and an apple.

Thursday morning she skipped her early walk to make the two-hour drive in a rented car to her parents' farm. In all the years she'd been away from home she'd never missed being on the farm on Thanksgiving. It was the holiday that most belonged to the farm. The arduous work of spring, summer and fall over, everyone, including the land itself, took a well-deserved rest.

Her father and her niece Betsy, Bob Junior's eldest daughter, met her near the bottom of the long driveway to the house. Verna rolled the window down.

"We saw the car and came out to see if it was you," Betsy explained excitedly. The air was so cold her words formed clouds of mist that floated above her long blond hair.

Verna put her hands out the open window and awkwardly embraced her niece. "Pop," she said when Betsy had moved away. Her father put his work-roughened hands in hers.

"Good to see you, Verna," he said with the half smile and wink he had always reserved for his youngest daughter.

Her father and Betsy walked beside the car as she drove slowly up the drive and parked at the end of the line of cars and pickup trucks that belonged to her six siblings.

"It *is* Verna," she heard her sister Shirley call as she came into the house. Soon she was surrounded and greeted by adults and children and dogs with thumping tails. Her mother came out of the kitchen, and the crowd parted to make room for her.

"Why, Verna," she exclaimed, "you're as brown as a berry and as thin as a rail."

"Hardly that thin," Verna replied as she received a warm hug in her mother's strong arms.

She was taken into the kitchen, steamy with roasting turkey, and fragrant with mince and pumpkin pies baked earlier in the day and now cooling on the counter. Her sisters and sisters-in-law resumed their tasks, and her mother offered coffee and a slice of warm apple cake to revive her after the trip. She accepted the coffee but turned down the cake. "Oh, Verna," her mother coaxed, "it's Thanksgiving. You don't have to diet on Thanksgiving."

"I'm saving my appetite for dinner," she replied tactfully. Her mother was an ample woman who enjoyed cooking and eating. She never had understood her daughter's desire to keep her weight under control.

Shirley came to Verna's defense. "Now, Mama, it's all right for us farm women to look like the broad side of a barn, but Verna needs something different. We've got to respect that." Her sister then asked if there was anything she wanted to eat or not to eat. Verna gratefully asked if they could hold the melted butter and cream sauce for the vegetables and serve them on the side.

"Well, that's simple enough," her mother replied skeptically as she handed Verna a bag of potatoes and a peeler.

Despite her best intentions, Verna ate too much turkey, potatoes and vegetables, and she couldn't resist one of her mother's homemade rolls and a small slice of pumpkin pie for dessert. Nor was the clatter and chatter of the twenty people around the table enough to keep her from thinking about Mel. He was about as different from her hardworking, clean-living, salt-of-the-earth family as anyone she could think of, but she knew he would get on with them well. He'd match Bob Junior pun for pun, romp with the toddlers, charm her parents with his wide-eyed curiosity. She tried a dozen times to put him out of her mind, but somehow he stayed with her, like a family member who couldn't make it home for the holidays.

After helping with the clearing up, she proposed a walk to her niece, who jumped at the chance to spend time alone with her favorite aunt. Betsy often said she wanted to be a lawyer, and Verna was more than happy to act as a role model for her niece. Leaving the farm had been tough for her because she was the first in the family to do it. She hoped the benefit of her experience would make whatever path Betsy eventually chose easier to follow. They tramped for more than an hour beside the stream that ran north of the house. Their cheeks were red, their feet icy when they finally got home.

In spite of her parents' protests, Verna left the farm early the next morning. There was too much to do in Des Moines for her to stay for the long weekend, but she promised to visit often while she was in the state and to spend a few days with them at Christmas before she went back to Washington.

The month flew by, and Verna didn't make as many visits home as she had hoped. She assuaged her guilt by telling herself that the work she was doing might eventually prove more important to her parents and other small farmers than the few hours she was unable to spend with them. But more than her work made her avoid the hominess of the farm. She could keep thoughts of Mel at bay when she was deep into the political process or agricultural policy, but in the warm atmosphere of home she missed him. She didn't like missing him. His memory was not the comfortable blur she had hoped it would become. It was altogether too sharp and clear.

Her hectic schedule made it difficult for her to adhere one hundred percent to the eating habits she had learned at the resort, but she got up early most mornings for a three-mile walk, and she used every trick she'd been taught for sticking as close as possible to her new eating patterns. Though managing her food and exercise routines was much more difficult, she still lost steadily. By the time she was about to return to Washington, her new smaller clothes were starting to feel loose in the waist and hips.

SHE ARRIVED in Washington late on a Thursday night in mid-January. On Friday she went shopping as soon as the stores opened. She spent the day cruising the Georgetown boutiques, combed nearly every rack in Neiman-Marcus and Saks Fifth Avenue and returned home with two stunning suits, a pair of chic daytime dresses, a sleek black overcoat, an evening outfit and all the necessary accessories. The clothes were the kind of high-fashion wear she had always dreamed of buying, but when she got them home, she decided that another radical change was required. She made a Saturday morning appointment at an exclusive salon, where she had a facial and a makeup session, and had her hair highlighted and cut in a shorter, layered style. The results were spectacular: she hardly recognized herself in the mirror.

On Monday morning she dressed very carefully for her return to the Hill, in a new suit of nubby beige wool flecked with gold. It had her first ever straight skirt, complete with a leg-revealing slit in the back. Under the collarless jacket she wore an off-white silk blouse with a soft bow-tie collar.

She looked so different from the woman who had left Washington two months earlier she was afraid the building guard wouldn't honor her identification pass. Luckily, the guard was one who knew her, although he did look at her pass twice before waving her on. She grinned to herself as she made a mental note to have her assistant make an appointment for a new ID photo.

As she walked in the door of her suite, the receptionist began to ask if she could help her, then realized it was Verna. "Ms Myers!" she exclaimed, then covered her embarrassment by stammering something about how nice it was to have her back in the office. Even her usually unflappable assistant raised a surprised eyebrow. "Funny," Jeanne Logan said to Verna imperturbably, "your voice didn't sound any different over the phone."

"I take it that's a compliment," Verna replied.

"It is. And here are your phone messages. It's been ringing off the hook already this morning. Jim Byram wants to see you ASAP, something about the ag bill. Shall I get his office for you?"

"Please." Verna went into her office and shut the door. She settled into her chair and started in on the enormous stack of catching up she had to do. Although she'd been in daily contact with Jeanne since returning from the resort, her prolonged absence would mean more than the usual amount of overtime. She had barely read a page when the buzzer sounded. Jim Byram was on the line.

"Welcome back!" His voice was as hearty and smooth as she had remembered it. Her heart sped up slightly. "I was just on my way to a committee meeting," he told her. "I've only got a minute, but there's something we need to work out on the ag bill. Can you have lunch? It's the only time I have open today. You shouldn't be booked on your first day back."

"I'm free," she confirmed, but she would have canceled almost anything for lunch with Jim.

"How about if I have some sandwiches sent up to your office?"

"Why don't we go out?" she countered. "I've been gone so long I'd like to see what's going on outside these four walls. With all the work on my desk this may be my only chance."

There was a second-too-long pause before he came back enthusiastically, "Sure, splendid idea. You pick the place. Have your office let my office know. See you later."

Verna made sure to arrive at the restaurant a few minutes late. She had never made an entrance before, but she wanted Jim to see her standing up before he saw her sitting down so that he'd know the change in her was more than a new hairstyle and new clothes. When she gave her name to the maître d', he told her that Congressman Byram was waiting at their table. He was reading a report as he waited and didn't see her approach. She had expected to feel excited and shaky. This was the moment she had planned for, had worked so hard for. But she felt strangely calm.

Her calm fled when she stood at the table and said hello. Jim raised his head from his report and began to greet her in an offhand manner. Suddenly his brain registered what his eyes were seeing, and he scrambled to his feet. "Verna? Verna!" He held out both hands to clasp hers. "You look, well, you look marvelous."

"You don't have to sound so surprised," she chided lightly. He was even more handsome and vibrant than she'd remembered. His shock of blond hair seemed thicker, his eyes so deep a blue they were almost violet. And they held a light she had never seen in them before.

The maître d' held her chair, and she sat down gratefully. She'd done it, she'd succeeded. Jim Byram wasn't looking at her like "good old Verna" anymore. The maître d' asked if she wanted something from the bar and she asked for a mineral water with a slice of lime.

"You must have had one helluva vacation," Jim commented. "Either that or you're in love." He raised a speculative eyebrow.

"The vacation *was* wonderful," she said, giving him what she hoped was a mysterious smile. Let him wonder about the falling-in-love part. She hadn't, but he didn't have to know that. Not right now.

"Tell me about it." He hadn't taken his eyes off her since she'd sat down. She hoped he never would.

Over broiled brook trout and salad she told him about her month at the resort. Of course she left out the part about Mel. He didn't have to know that the attentions of another man had been part of her marvelous transformation.

"I hate to say I told you so, but I do remember dropping a few pointed comments in the past about eating and exercise. I hope they may have had something to do with your decision to take this vacation."

"They may have," she said nonchalantly. "But there are some things one has to learn for one's self."

"There certainly are." Jim smiled with pleasure at what he saw.

Inside Verna was jubilant, but she wasn't ready to show him her excitement. Victory would be sweeter if she played it cool and let him come to her. "I know you didn't ask me to lunch to talk about my vacation, Jim. What's up?"

In order to get vote commitments for the bill he and Senator Carlsen were working on, he had had to make certain concessions, concessions to which the senator would be opposed. Jim explained the advantages of the changes and asked her to use her influence with the senator to make similar changes in the senate version of the bill.

"I need to know a lot more than you've told me. If I'm going to argue a case with the senator, I have to believe it's the right course myself. If I think it is, I'll do what I can. If not, you're on your own."

"That's all I wanted to hear. Tell me what you want and I'll have my office send it over this afternoon." He made a list of the documents she wanted to see and the people she wanted to have access to to check information. "Consider it done," he promised. "Thursday night I'm having dinner with Joe Halliday from the Department of Agriculture. It might be useful if you were there, too."

That Thursday evening, after Halliday left the restaurant where the three met, she and Jim lingered over their decaffeinated coffee and he asked to see her during the weekend. They met on Sunday afternoon for a cycle ride in Rock Creek Park and followed that with dinner. For the next three weeks they saw a lot of each other—professionally and unprofessionally. They were together so much that one of the town's gossip columnists speculated on the nature of their relationship in her column.

Verna loved going about town with Jim, being seen with him. But the relationship didn't fulfill her dreams of what it was going to be. More often than not she and

Jim talked business. Jim often held her hand or put an arm around her shoulders. He kissed her good-night warmly, but he was never more passionate than that. At first she had been glad he hadn't swept her away, as Mel had. For a while the anticipation of the caresses she felt were sure to come had been enough, but after three weeks she was beginning to wonder why Jim made no further advances. In all other ways he was decisive and went after what he wanted. She had thought many times that she wasn't what he wanted, but if that was true, why did he continue to see her outside work? The invitations always came from him, he included her in almost everything he did outside work. He must want to be with her. So she continued to see him, but her hopes for forging the perfect personal and political alliance became harder and harder to hold on to. And thoughts and dreams of Mel Hopkins continued to dog her.

When she first proposed Jim's changes in the bill to the senator, Agatha Carlsen shook her head impatiently. "Is this what Jim's been feeding you at those intimate little dinners I've been hearing so much about?"

With that question Verna realized she'd been naive about her senator. She had always supposed that Agatha Carlsen dismissed the personal gossip the rest of the town thrived on, but now she saw how wrong she'd been. Washington ran on information; no one who expected to operate in town could afford to dismiss any data before its value had been ascertained. She was hurt, however, that the senator thought she would take Jim's word for something just because she was seeing him outside work. She told Senator Carlsen what she'd

learned from talks with various experts, from the statistics and reports she'd studied. The senator argued
with her, pointed out problems and inconsistencies, but
in the end asked for more information.

All the time she was seeing him, Verna continued to
act as go-between for Jim and the senator. Finally, after
a month of wrangling and politicking, the bill was in a
form that both Agatha Carlsen and Jim Byram could
sponsor in their respective legislative chambers. Of
course, the work was far from over. There would be
amendments, deals made to ensure votes, the admin-
istration would have its reservations and additions, but
the bill was finally on its way to the floor.

As soon as that happened, Jim Byram seemed to
vanish as far as Verna was concerned. She didn't see or
hear from him from Monday to Friday. A few messages passed between his office and hers, but that was
all. He hadn't called her at home or asked her out for
the weekend. *He's probably going to Kansas this
weekend and forgot to tell me,* she rationalized. With
reelection every two years all members of the House
had to keep in frequent touch with their home dis-
tricts. But she was particularly disappointed not to have
heard from him. During the week she had finally
reached her goal weight. She had lost thirty-five pounds
and was eager to celebrate her achievement. *Next week,*
she told herself bravely, *next week Jim and I will celebrate.*

Work and personal chores kept her busy most of the
weekend, but the hours passed with no word from Jim,
and the feeling that something was very wrong grew
stronger and stronger. By Sunday evening she was

feeling very lonely and very angry. Jim could have called her to let her know his plans, she thought. True, they'd never said they weren't seeing other people, but they'd hardly been apart for a month. She had assumed... There they were again, those assumptions. She hated to think about what had happened the last time she'd made assumptions about a man. She broke their established pattern and called him at home. He answered on the first ring with a cheery hello.

"It's Verna."

"Hi, there," he answered nonchalantly. Then he paused, as if waiting for her to say something. She didn't. He might have the courtesy at least to ask how she was, she thought. Finally Jim said, "What can I do for you?"

"I, um, thought you might have gone home for the weekend."

"Nope."

"Oh. Well, um," she stammered, "I was wondering if you'd already had dinner. Maybe we could go out."

"Sorry," he said curtly. "I have other plans."

Suddenly it all made sense. The chaste hand-holding, the preemptive invitations. He had been using her to help him get what he wanted with the senator. Now he had gotten it. She was of no use to him anymore. "I take it those plans are permanent," she said coldly, "and do not include me."

His appreciative laugh made her blood boil. "That's what I like about you, Verna. You're one smart woman. You come right to the point. Aggie's taught you well."

"You could learn a few things from her, too. Manners, for a start, not to mention respect for other people's feelings."

"Don't start acting like a schoolgirl, Verna. You knew you weren't going to the high-school prom. This is the real world. You know how things work in this town. We had some good times. Where's the harm?"

She didn't like his condescending tone, but it made her see that she'd been a fool. She'd been taken in by him. Her next thought brightened her a little. There were little spots of egg on his face, too. "You know, Jim, I would have worked just as hard with you on the bill if you'd simply come to me and stated your case. If I hadn't been convinced your changes were good, I wouldn't have said a word to the senator, no matter how many times you took me out. It's too bad. You could have saved yourself a lot of unpleasant evenings squiring me around."

"But they weren't unpleasant at all," he protested mildly. "They're just over."

She had always admired Jim's cool, logical thinking. Now she saw that they went with a cold, logical heart. "Yes, they are. Goodbye, Jim." She hung up without letting him get in another word and started to pace her living room.

She'd never seen any deep feelings in him because he hadn't any, she fumed. He wasn't capable of any. Far better someone whose feelings spilled over like a too full jug than someone as cold and calculating as Jim. Mel Hopkins was a better man than Jim Byram ever would be, ever could be. Mel. She had never stopped missing

him. No matter how many corners she turned to es-
cape his memory, it always managed to follow her. Yet
she had lost him, made too many assumptions. She had
driven him away, thinking the grass would be greener
with Jim. Now she knew that the grass had been plenty
green with Mel, green and alive with feeling. She
couldn't understand how she could have ignored Jim's
lack of passion for so long. Next time she got involved
with a man she would know the difference right away.
If there was a next time . . .

Verna stopped pacing and flopped down on the
couch. She needed company, someone to talk to. She
called a friend who lived nearby and suggested dinner.
Her friend agreed, as long as she didn't have to change
out of her jeans and sweatshirt. They decided to meet
at a local beer-and-burger joint, where Verna suc-
cumbed to the temptation of a bowl of steak house fries.

That was only the first of many such slips.

12

"DO YOU WANT THAT?" Mel asked Jack Krynicki, eyeing the last piece of pepperoni pizza in the box they'd had delivered to the office.

"Take it." Jack leaned back in his swivel chair and put his feet up next to the keyboard on his desk. He took a swig from his beer bottle and crossed one worn running shoe over the other.

"It was too easy with Judy, right from the beginning. I should have suspected something." Mel tore into the piece of pizza with a vengeance.

"I'm your partner and your best friend, but I had no idea you were clairvoyant. When did you develop this astounding talent? Why have you been hiding it from me all this time?"

"Very droll, Krynicki."

"I know it must be a blow to the old ego, buddy, especially after what happened with Lana... Vera—"

"Verna," Mel supplied irritably.

"Right. But you found out Judy was more interested in your programs than your scintillating conversation before any real damage was done. It was three weeks ago, Mel. Let it go."

Jack had said that to him every day since they'd found out that Judy had breached security on their office computers, but it still rankled. He couldn't seem to get it right with women. Maybe he ought to stick with computers. "Hell's bells, Jack. An industrial Mata Hari, and I fell for it. It's just that Verna gave me such a hard time and Judy, well, fell right into my lap."

"So to speak," Jack said dryly.

"So to speak. You want to order another pizza?"

"Haven't you had enough?"

"Too much. But I want more, anyway."

"Didn't they tell you at that place that eating more than you need doesn't solve any problems? You must have put on four or five pounds already."

"Six. Of course they told us that eating is not a preferred method of problem-solving," Mel barked. "So I'm in a self-destructive, self-indulgent mood. So what? I'm not going to blow up like a blimp again."

"You are if you eat a pepperoni pizza every day."

"I'll stop when I feel better."

"Why don't you stop now? You'll feel better sooner."

"And why don't you stop lecturing me? I'm not a child of six."

"You're not?" Jack polished off his beer and stood. "I'm heading for home. Coming?"

"No, I'm going to stay here and work for a couple more hours."

Jack took his down parka off the hanger on the back of his door. "Don't stay here all night again. Go home, sleep in a bed for a change. It does wonders for the disposition."

"I don't want anything done to my disposition," Mel snapped.

"Suit yourself," Jack said mildly. "See you in the morning." He started to leave but turned back. "Why don't you give her a call?"

"Who?"

"You know, Velma."

"Verna! How come you know the names of the thousands of women you've dated but can't remember the name of my single solitary 'ex'?" Mel stormed.

"Aren't you forgetting Gillian?"

"See what I mean?" Mel tossed a wadded-up paper napkin at Jack, who caught it easily before it hit his face.

Jack grinned complacently. "I love it when you get mad."

Mel collapsed in his chair. "You really are intolerable sometimes."

"So are you."

"That must be the reason we get along so well."

"Must be. So why don't you call her? Verna, I mean."

"Thank you," Mel said with exaggerated courtesy. "What would I say? 'Hello, Verna? This is Mel. Remember me? The fat guy? I'm feeling bad because I fell for a woman who was being paid to find out what I was working on here at Peony Enterprises when I thought she really liked me and was interested in a serious long-term relationship and I'm drowning myself in pepperoni pizza because of it and would you like to marry me if you're not doing anything next weekend?'"

"That might work."

"Be serious, Jack."

Jack unzipped his parka and sat down again. "Just call her up, say you've been thinking about her and would she like to have dinner next weekend. If she says yes, you take her to a nice place, you see if you can get something going again. If you can't, forget it. You tried."

"You make it sound so simple. I can't let her see me like this."

"You're still thinner now than you were when you saw her last," Jack pointed out.

"That's not the point. The point is how I'm conducting my life."

"So you fell off the wagon. That doesn't mean you can't get back on."

"No, I suppose not," Mel reflected. He was silent for a moment. "You know what I'm going to do? I'm going to the resort for a refresher course, one of those long weekends they offer grads. When I get back, I'll call her. How's that sound?"

"Fine, if that's the way you want to handle it. The important thing is that you *do* handle it. You've been pining for that woman since the day you got back from the fat farm—"

"I wish you wouldn't call it that. It makes it sound like a place where they grow fat. And her name is Verna, not 'that woman,' not Vera, not Velma, not Lana."

"Excuse me. The weight-reduction spa where you met Verna," Jack amended, putting on a prissy voice.

"That's better."

"A spade is a spade is a spade," Jack paraphrased. "I still don't know why you let her go so easily. From what you told me, she seemed rather susceptible to more or less gentle persuasion."

"It seemed like a good idea at the time." Mel crushed the pizza box and threw it in the trash with a gesture of finality. "I'm serious, Jack. I'm going to call the resort in the morning, see if they've got a place for me. I'll fly down Thursday afternoon and come back on Sunday night. You can spare me for that long. I'll call Verna first thing when I get back. How does that sound?"

"Like I said, however you want to handle it, as long as you handle it. Now can I go home and get some sleep?"

"Sure. I think I'll come with you."

Jack's face lit up in a slow smile. "You really are serious, aren't you?"

"Yup."

"Hallelujah! I was getting real tired of pepperoni pizza."

"We could have had sausage or anchovy. All you had to do was speak up," Mel said as they left Jack's office.

"Now you tell me!"

MEL ARRIVED at the resort for dinner on Thursday night. He was greeted warmly by Carrie and introduced to some of the current clients, who were in the second week of their stay. He was heartened when he looked around the room. Despite his recent relapse to poor eating habits, he had kept up his exercise—he often ran the first four or five of Jack's daily ten miles with him—and he looked much more trim and fit than the people who had just begun to change their eating and exercise patterns.

Still, he had been right to come here. People like Jack who'd never carried an excess pound in their lives, who could easily run ten miles a day and eat whatever they pleased, didn't understand how difficult it was to change lifelong self-defeating habits. They often saw it as mere laziness and self-indulgence, when, in fact, the habits were deeply rooted in need, in the pain of loneliness or mistreatment or loss or grief. There was every reason to seek support, as he was doing, when something triggered a return to old habits.

Mel enjoyed his bowl of pasta with a chunky tomato sauce and went off to his room, not the same one he'd had before but virtually indistinguishable from it. He was glad he'd not been put either in his old room or in Verna's. The memories were strong enough in a place that merely looked like the rooms where they had spent so much time together. He spent the rest of the evening immersed in *Moby Dick*. The science fiction Verna had introduced him to had whetted an appetite for fiction. He had begun reading his way through all the classics he'd missed. He liked long Russian novels the best so far, but he'd read all of Tolstoy and Dostoyevski. Jack had recommended Melville. Besides *Moby Dick* he had brought along *Typee*, *Omoo* and *Billy Budd*. The four books ought to hold him for the weekend. He was a fast reader.

He woke early in the morning and decided to go for a short run on the beach before breakfast. He dressed quickly in his sweats, glad not to have to climb into the thermal underwear he found necessary for late-February running in Columbia. It was chillier on the island than it had been in November but still balmy compared to Maryland. He laced his running shoes, stretched for ten minutes and took off.

As he started out, he took deep gulps of the fresh salt air to cleanse his lungs and shake the last cobwebs of sleep from his brain. With his senses and brain fully operative he was completely taken in by the scenery. He watched the gulls swooping down to pick their breakfast out of the water, the waves rolling gently onto shore, the mist burning off on the horizon. Farther along the beach a solitary walker strode toward him. He stretched his arms high over his head and let out a loud whoop. He felt himself coming out of the bad patch. He was going to be all right. Everything was going to be all right. He whooped again. And again.

Verna was lost in her own thoughts as she walked the beach. She had wanted to get to the resort by dinnertime last night but hadn't been able to get away until late. She had arrived at midnight and gone straight to bed. She'd made sure to put her alarm clock on the bureau so that she'd have to get up to turn it off. She'd been feeling so tired lately that she sometimes slept through the alarm in the morning. But this morning she had awakened long before the alarm, more refreshed than she'd felt for weeks.

She'd taken what happened between her and Jim Byram very hard. She felt foolish and betrayed, angry at herself, angry at Jim. Though she confided in a couple of friends, she had no public redress. She still had to see him often at work. She had to suffer silently the speculation about why she and Jim were no longer the town's hottest couple. She took her refuge in food, to the point that her expensive new wardrobe was uncomfortably tight. A refresher weekend at the resort was definitely the right thing to do, she thought as she strode along. Even at the steep price it was cheaper than replacing her entire wardrobe.

She was amazed at her energy. She'd had the sense and willpower to keep up with her exercise, even though dragging herself out of bed for a brisk morning walk had been torture, especially in the cold weather. Today she loped along easily, arms swinging rhythmically, feet moving lightly. Merely being away from the heavy atmosphere that surrounded her in Washington had put a spring in her step.

A strange noise brought her out of her reverie. She looked overhead, thinking it had been the call of gulls, but saw no birds near her. The only other living creature on the beach was a jogger, a tall, well-built man with dark hair. Could he have been shouting? She heard the noise again. It carried down the beach on the wind, and she realized this time that it had indeed come from the jogger. His arms were raised over his head. He yelped again and turned around in a circle. *I wonder what he's so happy about*, she said to herself as she giggled at his antics.

Suddenly she stopped dead in her tracks. Her mouth fell open. The cavorting jogger was Mel Hopkins. What the devil was he doing on the beach? He *couldn't* have come to the resort for a refresher weekend, too. She must be mistaken. But the runner had come several yards closer now. She could see his face. It definitely was Mel.

Her breath caught in her throat, half excitement, half trepidation. Involuntarily her feet began moving backward. But trying to run away was useless. The resort was in the other direction, and besides, he'd catch up with her soon enough, anyway. She could try keeping her head very low as she passed him, but that was silly. They'd see each other soon enough at the resort, anyway. She started walking quickly toward him. She might as well get it over with. Say "hello, how are you" and get on with her walk.

Mel stopped yelling and dancing and continued his run. He could see now that the approaching walker was a woman, a blonde. She looked vaguely familiar from this distance, a bit like Verna. But Verna's hair was darker and longer, and for exercising she always pulled it into a ponytail. He'd loved that ponytail, flopping girlishly behind her head. No, the woman couldn't be Verna. What would she be doing here? He must be doing some wishful thinking, powerful wishful thinking, for with every step the woman seemed more and more like Verna.

At twenty yards he was sure. It *was* Verna. She'd done something to her hair and she'd lost some more weight since he'd last seen her, but it definitely was her. His heart seemed to leap, and he raced toward her, waving his arms and shouting her name.

Oh, no, he's seen me, Verna thought in a panic. But her reservations crumbled as he loped toward her like a puppy just let off the leash. She raised her hand and waved back, tentatively at first and then with more and more enthusiasm.

How she had missed him!

13

"VERNA! VERNA! VERNA! What are you doing here?" Mel kept jogging in place when he reached her, unable to stop moving because he was so excited.

"Right now I'm taking a walk. I, um, gained back a few pounds." She didn't want to get into the whole miserable business with him, so she brightened her tone. "I thought a refresher course could get me back on the right track. So here I am."

"You look fabulous to me."

"I do?" She pushed her hair off her forehead self-consciously. For the past few weeks all she'd been able to think of every time she looked in the mirror was how tired and drab she seemed.

"You've done something to your hair. I like it. It makes you look—oh, I don't know—softer or something. I'm not good at saying things like this. All I know is that it looks great to me."

"Thanks. I had it cut. And what they now call high-lighted. That's just a highfalutin term for bleached blonde. For the price the salon charges they have to call it something fancy."

They laughed together. Mel wanted to take her in his arms and hug her tight, but he deliberately took a step back instead. If anything was going to happen between them again, he couldn't push her, push them.

Verna thought for a moment he was going to reach out and hold her, but then he moved away. *He's probably found someone else by now*, she thought. *He's so darned good-looking.* The lines and planes of his face were sharper, more pronounced, but he hadn't lost his boyish freshness. The combination was irresistible. She shivered slightly. "Could we move on? It's a little chilly to be standing here."

"Sure, okay, anything you want." They began to walk in the direction of the resort, and an awkward silence fell between them.

"How have you been?" Mel asked after a while.

"Not so bad," Verna answered. "Yourself?"

"Hangin' in there." They took a few more paces. "By the skin of my teeth, that is," Mel muttered under his breath.

"I know what you mean," she admitted.

"So we've both been pretty lousy. That's why we're here, but neither of us wants to talk about it, right?"

"I'd say that's a fair assessment of the situation."

They walked another hundred yards in silence.

"Pepperoni pizza," Mel said.

"Bacon cheeseburgers, fries drowned in catsup," she replied.

"I couldn't stop myself," they said in unison.

They looked at each other in surprise for a moment and then started to laugh, tentatively at first.

"Banana splits," Mel said. They both laughed a bit harder.

"Chocolate cake. Whole ones." This prompted renewed gales of giggles.

"Giant double bags of potato chips."

"Vats of hot buttered popcorn."

They were both laughing hysterically now. "Mayonnaise sandwiches," Mel sputtered.

"For the truly desperate," Verna said between peals.

Their laughter died down, and they stood on the beach gasping for breath. "Whew! That felt good," Verna exclaimed when she had calmed down enough to speak clearly again.

"I tried to explain it to Jack—you remember, my partner—but he doesn't understand. With you I only have to name a food in a certain tone of voice and you know exactly what I mean. Oh, it *is* good to see you again, Verna."

"And you, Mel," she said quietly.

Back at the resort they ate a breakfast of whole-grain cereal with skim milk and banana slices. Mel told Verna about all the books he'd been reading and how it was all due to her that he'd even started reading fiction at all. He went on at length about Russian novels, as enthusiastic as if he'd discovered and published them himself.

Verna thoroughly enjoyed Mel's zesty conversation. By comparison he made Jim Byram look a cold fish indeed. How had she ever let herself be taken in by him? He put on a good show but was very short on substance. Why hadn't she seen that until he pointed it out so bluntly? But all that was over, she reminded herself. She had to stop thinking about it. "You talk about the Karamazov brothers as if they were members of your family."

"In a way they are," he replied. "It's been fun meeting all these new 'people.'"

"Russia's a big country, with big books," she said with a grin. "You must have made a lot of friends."

"Real people are better. Especially old friends."

He smiled nostalgically at her, and she thought of their many hours together, days of laughter, nights of lovemaking. "Yes, they are."

After breakfast they went their separate ways, both needing some time to get used to the idea of the other being around. They saw one another during the day, chatting between classes, getting reacquainted. After dinner Verna suggested they go into town to hear a bluegrass band at a club she'd seen advertised on the resort's bulletin board.

Throughout the evening the conversation never lagged, but neither volunteered any information about the events that had sent each of them back to the resort. They were testing the waters like bathers on a Maine beach in July. They might need relief from the hot sun, but the water was too cold to plunge right in.

After the concert Mel walked her to her door. "Will I see you in the morning?" he asked.

"I'll be here," she promised.

"How about a walk before breakfast?"

"Sure. Seven-thirty?"

"Fine."

They took long searching measure of each other until Mel raised his hand and brushed it slowly across her cheek. His simple touch was like a spark that lit a coal she had long ago given up on rekindling. But now the coal was relit, smoldering insider her. It was a feeling much like missing him had been, only warmer, more hopeful, less forlorn.

"I'll see you in the morning, Verna. Sleep well."

"I will."

Inside she undressed slowly and climbed into a silky powder-blue nightgown, one of the new ones she'd treated herself to when she reached her goal weight, which had been the same week that Jim dumped her. She wasn't sure she'd ever need the new nightgowns, but she wore them, anyway, and left her comfy flannel nightclothes packed away in a rarely used suitcase. But now that she'd run into Mel, she thought she might not have bought the gowns in vain. It was funny, she thought, as she creamed off her makeup and brushed her hair, *both of us showing up here.* It must be fate, she told herself, feeling almost giddy with anticipation. For she knew he was still interested in her, that his feelings hadn't disappeared any more than hers had. Why, she wondered, hadn't she noticed the strength of those feelings when she was in the throes of them?

She thought she heard a tapping at the door and listened closely. It stopped. *Must have been the wind or something,* she decided. But then she heard it again. There was someone knocking at the door. She put on her robe—a blue-flowered kimono—and went to the door. "Who is it?" she called softly.

"Mel. Are you ready?"

"Ready for what?" Verna opened the door a crack. He was standing there in sweats and sneakers.

"Didn't we agree to go for a walk at seven-thirty?" He held out his wrist and pointed to his multipurpose chronometer. The digital characters said it was seven-thirty on Saturday morning.

Verna held back her laughter. It was just like him to do something like this. "Sorry, I must have overslept. Can you wait a minute while I slip into something more suitable for walking?"

"Do you have to?"

"I can't very well go walking dressed like this, can I?"

"You could try."

"I'll only be a minute." She shut the door in his face. Ha! she crowed to herself. Two could play at this game. She changed hastily into sweats and sneakers and opened the door again.

"That was quick."

"I didn't want to keep you waiting."

"Woods or beach?" he asked. Neither of them gave any hint that they were doing anything unusual.

"Woods."

"Good choice." Mel picked up the emergency beam he'd gotten from the reception desk of the resort. The lamp was powerful enough to make them feel they had their own personal sun lighting their path. They set off at a brisk pace.

"Sleep well?" Verna asked.

"Like a baby. I always say there's nothing like a good night's sleep followed by a bracing walk."

But for the crunching of their shoes on the pebbly path the night was absolutely still. There were no lights anywhere and they seemed to be the only creatures stirring. As they got deeper into the woods, the path was covered by a carpet of pine needles and all they heard was their own breathing. The night air was cold enough to condense their breath into a fine mist as they exhaled.

"I was going to call you when I got back from the resort," Mel said quietly, speaking barely above a whisper. The night silence commanded respect.

"Were you?" She smiled into the darkness. Fate may have brought them here together this weekend, but knowing that Mel had plans to give fate a hand made her feel quite breathless.

"Yes. I don't know why I haven't called you before this. And I'm not sure now why I let our relationship end when we left the resort. But I didn't and I did, if you see what I mean, and now I want to make up for that, if I can, if you'll let me, if you want me to, that is. I'm babbling."

"Like a brook." She heard his soft laughter, and her giddiness turned to boldness. "Why did you let things end so easily? I expected you to be more, er, persuasive."

"I guess I was tired of fighting for you. Tilting at windmills pales after a while. I wanted you to come to me, willingly. I didn't think you would do that. Would you have kept things going if I'd asked you to?"

"I don't know," she answered honestly. "I was pretty confused then."

"And now?"

"Things are starting to clear up."

They tramped along in silence for a quarter mile, then Mel said, "I had a pretty rotten experience after I left here. With a woman, I mean. It sent me right to the pepperoni pizzas."

"Join the club," she said wryly.

"You, too?" He looked at her with surprise.

"Did you think you'd taken out the patent on fool-ishness?"

"No, I guess not." But, he thought to himself, she always seemed so sure of herself, so much in control. Then again there had to have been some reason for her to come back to the resort. He had assumed it was something to do with her high-pressure job. Maybe it wasn't.

"Why don't you tell me about it?" Verna suggested.

Mel felt less like a sap knowing that she'd had a similar experience. That made it easier to tell about meeting Judy, about her pursuing him, about the blow to his ego—personal and professional—when he'd found out she was only after what was in his brain, not what was in his heart.

"I sympathize, Mel, I really do," she said after he'd finished his story. "But at least you have the satisfaction of knowing that you were a victim only to someone else's betrayal, not to your own self-sabotage." She went on to tell him about how she'd come to the resort to get thin enough and athletic enough to entice a certain congressman. She hadn't counted on meeting Mel. "And I didn't let you stand in the way of my plans, no matter how much happened between us. So back I went to Washington where I found that my plan had succeeded. The congressman not only noticed me, he started taking me out. But as soon as he'd gotten what he wanted from me, he dumped me. I guess it was good that it happened that way," she concluded, thinking aloud. "You see, I'd have worked just as hard for the compromise bill if he hadn't been dating me. But if I hadn't gone out with him, I'd still be sitting back in

Washington pining for him, instead of walking here with you."

"Are you glad to be walking here with me?" Mel asked, his voice taut with emotion.

"Yes," she answered readily. "I missed you."

Mel stopped walking and put the lamp down on the ground. The beacon shone directly up into their faces, lighting them as if it were day. "Did you?" he asked, his smile sending out as bright a beam as the lamp's.

Verna looked up at him and nodded. The strength of her feelings about him were as clear and radiant as the light from the lamp that lit their path. How hard she had worked to deny those true feelings, she realized as they enveloped her, filling her inside and out with a shining warmth.

Mel reached out and gently cupped her face in his hands. "For two smart people we've been pretty dumb," he said, caressing her cheeks in small circles with his thumbs.

"Mistakes are an important part of the learning process, or so I'm told." Her breath seemed to be caught in her throat and it was difficult to get the words out.

He reached up to touch her hair, run his fingers through it. "I do love your hair like this," he said huskily. He bent slowly and placed his lips gently on hers.

The taste of him was familiar and deeply comforting, like the special foods her mother had made for her when she was sick as a child. He warmed her, cossetted her, made the last of the hurt disappear.

Their lips were the only thing that touched. Both held back, moving slowly from words to physical expression of their happiness in being reunited. They stood back after the tender kiss and took a long deep drink from one another's eyes, a drink that whetted their thirst for each other.

"Let's go back," Mel said quietly. "I have a lot more things I'd like to say to you. In private."

Hand in hand they walked back to Verna's room, slowly, deliberately. There was no need to hurry, for they were in their own time zone, where they created day or night, where the passing of minutes or hours was measured not by some arbitrary standard but in the joy and delight they shared.

14

VERNA CLOSED THE DOOR to her room softly behind them. Swiftly Mel's arms closed around her. With a whoop he picked her up and whirled her around the room. "This is a lot easier than it used to be," he wise-cracked.

"And not as easy as it's going to be." She wrapped her arms around his neck and let her head fall back and the room spin around her. It had been a struggle to keep her feet on the ground lately. Now it felt wonderful to let go completely, to know and trust that she was supported.

When Mel finally put her down, she was breathless and dizzy, but she didn't mind. It was as if her head had been cleared of a mess of dusty old cobwebs. She leaned limply against his chest.

"I'm so happy I've found you again." Mel kissed the top of her head and held her close. "And I'm happy it was here, where we first met, in a place where we both felt we could come to recoup and regroup."

"I know I didn't consciously expect to find you here, but I wasn't entirely surprised, either. You seem so much a part of this place. So much a part of me," she added quietly. "I don't know why I didn't realize it before. I guess because it wasn't part of my 'best laid schemes.'"

"Don't put all the blame on yourself," Mel chided. "I was the one who let you go, who decided to stand on my pride at the last moment. I should have gone on making a fool of myself over you. At least it would have been honest. I am absolutely gaga over you, and what's more, I have been from the first moment I saw you. It was like lightning had struck when you stepped out of your car and started to yell at me for passing you on the road."

"Passing me! Almost running me off it is more accurate," she protested.

"Whatever," Mel said easily, putting a quiet finger on her lips. "The important thing is how I felt. How I feel. How I will feel."

"And how is that?"

"I won't always feel the way I do now. I'll feel more strongly about you. I know that." He pressed his lips to hers so that she got a very clear picture of how he felt about her at that moment. She couldn't imagine a kiss more fervent, more expressive, but she knew she'd like to be around when they were invented. "Would you do something for me?" he asked when he released her.

"Mmmm," she murmured, lifting her head to plant a small series of kisses on his face that were like the aftershocks that came with an earthquake.

"Change into whatever it was you were wearing before we went for our walk."

"Would you like that?" She caressed his face with her fingertips, curled an unruly lock of hair behind one ear.

"Very much."

She left his arms slowly, able to let him go only because of the promise of better things to come. "I won't be long."

She went into the bathroom and changed back into her nightgown. Before she put her robe on, she dabbed drops of her favorite perfume behind her ears and between her breasts. She bent over from the waist and brushed her hair up from the nape of her neck. When she stood, she shook it to settle it on her head but did little else to disturb the wild, almost wanton, look of it. Satisfied with her appearance, she wrapped her robe about her, belted it loosely and went into the bedroom.

She found Mel propped up in bed waiting for her, the covers pulled up to his waist, his naked chest above them. He smiled and held out his hands when she appeared in the doorway. "Now I see what took you so long," he murmured.

"Was it long?" Verna asked as she crossed the room. She stood at the edge of the bed and took his hands in hers.

"It seemed like forever to me. But it was worth it." He moved over to make room for her on the bed. She sat next to him, and he put his arm around her shoulders. "This is where we belong, Verna, all tucked up and cozy together."

"It *is* nice, isn't it?" She snuggled up to him and laid her head on his bare chest. Through the warm flesh she could hear the steady beat of his heart, the metronome that beat out a rhythm of pure happiness.

They sat close and quiet for a long while. Being together needed no embellishments, no talk, no caresses.

Breathing the same air, hearts beating in the same rhythm was enough. For a time.

The closeness had its effect on both of them. They needed to become closer, to blend, melt into one. Mel's breathing began to quicken; Verna's raced in response. He reached down and loosened the belt of her robe. Then he slipped his hand inside the opened garment, grazing the tip of her breast. She drew a sharp breath at his touch. It was the merest meeting of flesh, but it sent a jolt of excitement jumping through her.

He pushed the robe off her shoulders, then sat back to look at her. Her entire body tingled as he raked his eyes over her from head to foot. "I thought you were the most beautiful woman I'd ever seen the first night I made love to you. Now you're a different woman and you're even more beautiful, even though you're the same person. If you see what I mean. It's mind-boggling."

Verna blushed becomingly. "It's hard to believe anything would boggle your mind."

"You do." He caressed her buttock and buried his face in her neck, kissing and nipping at it.

She leaned back against the pillows, luxuriating in the heat of his hand through the flimsy material of her gown. His hands moved up her sides and grasped her shoulders. He raised his head and crushed his mouth to hers. His tongue darted tantalizingly between her parted lips, found hers and played a breathtaking game with it, circling and feinting and touching.

They were both breathing hard and fast when he let her go. He took hold of the straps of her gown and gently lowered them. The gown slipped lower on her already half-bare breasts, exposing the top circle of her nipples. He ran the back of his hand over her bare flesh and she gasped.

"Steady," he whispered as he lifted her arms through the straps of her gown and lowered it to her waist. He bent and took one breast into his mouth, caressing the other with his hand. She moaned softly and wrapped her arms around his neck. He toyed with her nipples until they'd hardened and she was transported to that twilight zone between arousal and ecstasy. She whispered his name; he looked up at her and smiled. "I'm here," he assured her.

"I'm well aware of that," she said with a lopsided grin.

He slid out from under the covers and knelt beside her. He eased her nightgown over her waist and hips and legs, following the fabric with a trail of hot, moist kisses. Then he retraced his path, starting at the ankles. Every spot he touched with his lips burned like a place in the forest hit by summer heat lightning. The fire soon caught and raged throughout the rest of Verna's body.

She sizzled when he buried his face in the hot juncture of her thighs. He explored her wet, aching center, and she cried out with ecstasy and need. She grasped his shoulders, feeling she would fly out of the universe if she didn't hold on to him. He continued to excite her until she felt she stood at the edge of an endless black precipice. She cried out again and tugged at his shoulders.

He responded slowly, inching and kissing his way up from her center until he was poised over her. She opened her eyes and found him looking back at her with passion and longing and tenderness. "I love you," he whispered.

The voice that came in response sounded from the depths of her. "I love you," she affirmed. She reached out and found him, gloriously erect. His eyes stayed fast on hers as she guided him into her and they merged.

She clasped him fast as he settled into her, filling her, fulfilling her with his long, strong strokes, bringing her once again to the edge of that same black precipice. She was afraid to go over the edge, afraid she might shatter. But he urged her on, teasing her, pleasing her, until she had no choice but to fall into the darkness. As she tumbled, she burst into shards of sparkling, shimmering light. She called his name over and over, for each dazzling piece of her had his name written on it.

He grasped her buttocks and plunged deep and hard into her. She opened herself to accept him fully, unconditionally. He took her faster and faster; harder, harder, deeper, deeper, until he stiffened, paused for a long moment and drove himself home with a cry. His hot flesh pulsed rapidly as he emptied his strength, his love, his self into her.

He lay absolutely still for a moment, not even breathing. She felt his weight, glad to bear it, for it was solid and real. Then he began to breathe again, heavy heaving breaths that gradually settled down. He propped himself on his elbows and grinned down at her. "I hadn't realized how much I missed you."

"How much was that?" she asked, brushing a curl from his dampened forehead.

"I could show you all over again, but I think I'd have to wait another four or five months."

"Nothing doing," she said quickly.

He settled himself next to her and cuddled her. "You'd prefer me to stick around?"

"Infinitely."

"I wouldn't mind doing just that. If you'll have me, that is."

She sat up and stared down at him, full of joy. She hoped he meant what she thought he meant. "Would you mind repeating that?" she asked with some trepidation, just in case he hadn't meant what she thought he'd meant.

"Not at all."

Mel sat up and took her hand in his. "Will you marry me, Verna?" he asked simply.

So many questions went through her mind—where would they live? how would it work? would they have children?—but she managed to silence her overactive brain. She wanted to be with him, share her life with him. The rest of it was details. Those could be worked out. "Yes," she answered.

He looked stunned for a moment. Then he sprang to his knees. "You will! Really?"

"Of course," she said.

"Wha-hoooooo!" he yodeled. He jumped off the bed and ran around to the other side. He pulled her up and into a bone-crushing bear hug that took her breath away.

"If you kill me," she choked out, "I won't be able to marry you."

He put her down and apologized with a laugh. "I'm so excited I hardly know what I'm doing, what I should do."

"You should settle down," she advised, "and get back into bed. And under the covers. It's chilly out here in the altogether."

They burrowed into the bed together, holding each other tight. "When? Where? How? Where shall we live? How many kids will we have?" Mel fired the questions at her in rapid succession.

"Slow down," she said, ruffling his hair. "I hear you have to have staying power in a marriage."

They talked the rest of the night away, making and discarding plans until they settled on a course of action. They'd marry in the spring in Iowa. First they'd find and furnish a house in a suburb halfway between Columbia and Washington, which they'd move into after the wedding. After they got used to being married, they'd think about additions to the family.

"What if I decide I want to run for office? We'd have to go back to live in Iowa. What about your business?"

"What's the problem? Is there some law against having computers in Iowa?"

Verna smiled sheepishly. "No, we're very advanced about that in Iowa."

"Then I can work in Iowa. I just happened to be in Columbia because when Jack and I decided to go into business, the city offered us a lot of attractive incentives to set ourselves up there. But I can work anywhere. What's inside my head is important, not my address."

"What about Jack?" she asked.

"If you have computers in Iowa, you must have tele-
phones, too."

"We've had them for a long time."

"I thought so."

He took her into his arms then and demonstrated
some of the staying power she'd mentioned earlier. As
the first light crept into the room, they fell into a deep,
exhausted sleep.

VERNA WAS ROUSED by a faraway pounding sound. As
she rose from the depths of sleep, she identified it.
Someone was knocking on the door. Squinting against
the strong light that poured into the room, she glanced
at the bedside clock. It was after nine. They'd overslept and missed breakfast. Not surprising, she thought
as she gathered her robe and her wits. They'd only been
asleep for a few hours.

The knocking continued, and now she heard someone calling her name. "Coming," she called out. Mel
didn't stir. She pecked him fondly on the cheek and left
the bedroom, shutting the door behind her.

She found Carrie on the other side of the door. "I'm
sorry to disturb you, but we were a little worried. You
weren't at breakfast and you didn't answer your phone."

She hadn't even heard the phone ring. "Sorry." She
began to mumble something about hard work and too
little sleep.

Inside the bedroom Mel woke with a start. The first
thing he realized was that Verna was gone. He jumped
out of bed. *She's done another bunk on me*, he thought
fuzzily. "Damn it, I thought we had everything
straightened out last night," he muttered to himself.

"Why does she keep doing things like this to me? She can't. I won't let her." He ripped open the door, stormed into the living room. "Verna!" he yelled.

Not until he saw Carrie in the doorway did he remember he was stark naked. "Oh, hell!" he exclaimed, then doubled over and beat a hasty retreat into the bedroom.

Simultaneously Verna and Carrie began to apologize profusely, Carrie for intruding, Verna for Carrie having been embarrassed. Neither could hear anything the other had to say. They stopped talking at the same time and looked away in mortification. Then suddenly Verna began to laugh. She tried to stop herself, but it was impossible. The thought of Mel doubling over and backing out of the room was just too funny.

Once Verna started, Carrie couldn't contain herself. She giggled self-consciously and allowed herself several tension-relieving guffaws.

"I'm really sorry," Verna said when they'd quieted down.

"These things happen," Carrie said. She lowered her voice. "I'm really glad to see you and Mel together. You're a terrific couple. Two of my best success stories. And with Mel, now I know exactly how much of a success."

Carrie and Verna grinned at each other conspiratorially. "If we'd been such successes," Verna said, "we wouldn't have had to come back here. And we might not have found each other again."

"Just as I said. Two of my best success stories. I'm glad to see the saga continues. I hope it runs for a long time." Carrie gave Verna a quick hug. "If you hurry, you can make yoga class."

"Where we can get in some practice for tying ourselves in a knot," Verna said somewhat cryptically.

Carrie looked confused for a moment, then her face lit up. "You're getting married! Congratulations!" She gave Verna another bigger hug. "Great news, Mel!" she sang out in a loud voice. "I'll see you both later. This is so exciting," she gushed as she rushed off.

"You can come out now," Verna called.

The door opened slowly, and Mel, dressed in his sweats, slunk out into the living room. "What was Carrie doing here?" he asked feebly.

"What were you doing charging around like a mad rhinoceros?"

"I woke suddenly and you were gone. I thought you'd gotten scared and run off again, like that first night. I acted on impulse."

Verna went to him and wrapped her arms around him. "This is my room," she reminded him gently.

"I didn't think of that until afterward." He held her close and kissed the top of her head. "I don't want to lose you. Ever."

"You won't. You're stuck with me."

"I hope so." He kissed her deeply. "I love you so much," he murmured against her cheek.

"I won't be running away anymore, Mel. I love you too much for that."

"What if we have a big fight or something?" He held her even more closely, as if that could prevent anything from ever coming between them.

"We're bound to disagree and have arguments sometimes." Verna pushed herself away from him gently. "But let's make a deal."

"What kind of deal?" He took one of her hands in his and brought it to his lips.

"If ever one of us simply has to get away from the other for a few days, for whatever reason, we'll come to only one place. Here." She brought the hand that was holding hers to her cheek and pressed it there. "But only as a last resort," she said with a smile.

"Only as a last resort," he agreed as he took her in his arms and kissed her greedily.

"We'll be late for yoga," she murmured.

"Let's skip it. We can stay here and invent our own positions." He started to back her into the bedroom. "Heck, maybe we can invent our own diet and exercise program."

"Frequent sex and no food?"

"We could try it until lunchtime. See how it works out."

He kicked the bedroom door shut behind them. "I think it's going to work just fine." He removed her robe and let it flutter to the floor. His sweats came off in a minute. They climbed into bed and into one another's arms.

From that moment they were with each other, for each other, first, last, forever.

Harlequin Temptation

COMING NEXT MONTH

Six exciting series for you every month... from Harlequin

Harlequin Romance·
The series that started it all

Tender, captivating and heartwarming...
love stories that sweep you off to faraway places
and delight you with the magic of love.

◆

Harlequin Presents·

Powerful contemporary love
stories...as individual as the
women who read them

The No. 1 romance series...
exciting love stories for you, the woman of today...
a rare blend of passion and dramatic realism.

◆

Harlequin Superromance®
It's more than romance...
it's Harlequin Superromance

A sophisticated, contemporary romance-fiction
series, providing you with a longer,
more involving read...a richer mix of complex plots,
realism and adventure.

Harlequin
American Romance™
Harlequin celebrates the American woman...

...by offering you romance stories written about American women, by American women for American women. This series offers you contemporary romances uniquely North American in flavor and appeal.

◆

Harlequin Temptation™
Passionate stories for today's woman

An exciting series of sensual, mature stories of love...dilemmas, choices, resolutions... all contemporary issues dealt with in a true-to-life fashion by some of your favorite authors.

◆

Harlequin Intrigue™
Because romance can be quite an adventure

Harlequin Intrigue, an innovative series that blends the romance you expect... with the unexpected. Each story has an added element of intrigue that provides a new twist to the Harlequin tradition of romance excellence.

Harlequin Books®

PROD-A-2

ATTRACTIVE, SPACE SAVING BOOK RACK

Display your most prized novels on this handsome and sturdy book rack. The hand-rubbed walnut finish will blend into your library decor with quiet elegance, providing a practical organizer for your favorite hard-or soft-covered books.

Only $9.95

Approximately 16" x 8" when assembled

Assembles in seconds!

To order, rush your name, address and zip code, along with a check or money order for $10.70* ($9.95 plus 75¢ postage and handling) payable to *Harlequin Reader Service*:

Harlequin Reader Service
Book Rack Offer
901 Fuhrmann Blvd.
P.O. Box 1396
Buffalo, NY 14269-1396

Offer not available in Canada.

*New York and Iowa residents add appropriate sales tax.

BKR-1A